THE SONS OF CHAOS: VALI AND NARFI LOKISON

THE SONS OF LOKI

J. L. BUTLER

PROLOGUE

In Old Norse mythology, Loki is the immortal god of Chaos. According to myth Loki married the goddess Sigyn and they produced two sons whom they named Narfi and Vali. In my book, "Loki and Sigyn: A Love Story", Vali and Narfi are born in the time of the Vikings. In the following series about "The Sons of Loki", these twin boys have lived for hundreds of years on into contemporary times. They have inherited their magical abilities from their Sorcerer father as well as Loki's penchant for mischief. The series follows Vali and Narfi as they grow from adolescents in Asgard, the home of the gods, into young adulthood.

My first book, "Loki and Sigyn: A Love Story", gave the reader an alternative look at what might have happened had Loki and Sigyn met as children in the magnificent Realm of Asgard. It explored the typical trials and tribulations of adolescents anywhere. The difference was that these adolescents were gods who possessed extraordinary powers. In my opinion, Loki was wrongly vilified in Norse Mythology. I think the other gods were jealous of him because he was said to be the most intelligent and the most attractive of all the gods. I believe he was a prankster because he was smart enough to get away with it and attractive enough to be easily forgiven. In the end, Loki finally went too far and met a horrible end at the hands of the Aesir (Asgardian gods).

In my research of Norse Mythology I got the feeling that Odin was behind all of the ill treatment heaped upon Loki. It was said that Odin had knowledge of the future and in order for his visions to come true he had to make Loki become the architect of Ragnarok (the Norse equivalent of Armageddon). As I see it, Odin drove Loki to the point where he verbally attacked the other gods so viciously that they condemned him to be tied to a rock by his son's entrails until the end of time. His loyal wife Sigyn saved Loki from the additional torment of the drip of snake's venom onto his face by holding a bowl between her husband and the snake. At Ragnarok Loki broke free and was instrumental in destroying Asgard and bringing death to all of its gods.

I looked at this and wondered, "What if someone had interceded? What if Odin had gotten it all wrong? What if Ragnarok didn't have to happen?" I gave Loki and his family a different fate in "Loki and Sigyn". I realize that I have taken a lot of liberties with Norse Mythology, but I think the subsequent adventures are much more satisfying. You probably won't enjoy these books if you're a serious student of Norse Myths and Legends but if you're a fan of Fantasy with a little Science Fiction thrown in, I think you'll really enjoy the series, "The Sons of Loki".

The first of the series, "The Sons of Chaos: Vali and Narfi Lokison (The Sons of Loki)", I have Vali and Narfi as teenagers in Asgard. As explained in "Loki and Sigyn", the boys were forced to spend their early childhood banished to Siberia along with their mother. As immortals their childhood lasted hundreds of Earth years but by Asgardian standards they were like typical children aged nine or ten. By the time I reintroduce them in "The Sons of Chaos", they had reached Asgardian adolescence, which took another hundred years or so of Earth time. This accounts for the fact that they were born in the Twelfth Century but were aware of events on Earth that happened in the early Twentieth Century. As immortals their story is timeless. In subsequent books about "The Sons of Loki", you will see them as young adults. I have made the aging process among the Aesir come almost to a halt by the age of Asgardian "majority".

I hope you will enjoy these "new" mythological characters as much as I have. I thought that Loki and his family deserved a better story than the one written for them in

Old Norse Mythology. These books are my attempt to give it to them.

    Enjoy.

(May the Chaos be with you…)

CHAPTER 1

The boys had been raised in a frozen wilderness. Their only other contacts had been their mother and an old teacher of hers from her homeland. Their mother had not been married to their father; she had, in fact, been married to another man when they were conceived. They knew they possessed noble blood, that their true father was a Prince of the Royal Family, but never felt such distinction made them in any way privileged. It was simply a fact. The discovery of the affair between their mother and father had resulted in their banishment from Asgard to Siberia, on the planet Earth, of the realm of Midgard. Their parents were Loki, the god of Mischief and son of Odin, and the goddess Sigyn. The two had fallen in love as children, only to be most cruelly torn apart in the name of political expediency.

The boys were identical twins and none save their mother and father could tell them apart. Hundreds of years old in Earth years, they were mere adolescents among the immortals of Asgard. Like their father, they were sorcerers extraordinaire. Their talents almost rivaled those of their powerful father, but they had been taught from an early age to keep their abilities in check. Loki chose to use his power only as a last resort, preferring to use the power of his intellect over that of his magic whenever possible. Sigyn had insisted the children do the same and they did, for the most part. They were, after all, still boys, although in adolescence, it might be said they stood on the brink of manhood.

Thanks to Syr, the old teacher of Loki and Sigyn while they both lived in the Castle of Asgard, the boys learned of a way to return to the city and to retrieve their father. Narfi, the younger of the two by approximately three minutes, possessed the more adaptable and subtle skills of sorcery so the decision was made that he should go to Asgard alone. His brother Vali, still a very capable sorcerer, stayed with his mother and Syr as their protector while Narfi was away. Narfi found his father, who had been living with the lie told to him that his family was dead. Other lies were revealed and the ultimate lie, the one in which Odin believed he saw the only inevitable path to the future, lay uncovered by Syr. Odin, forced by Syr to envision different paths into the future had since ceased to try to manipulate the circumstances of the day to fit his limited sight. As a result, Loki and his family finally reunited with the Asgardians, and Odin handed the crown to Thor.

Loki had not always set the best example. The day after their return to Asgard, there was a great feast planned to celebrate the return of the banished Thor and Loki's family of Sigyn and the boys. As Tyr, one of Loki's biggest detractors, stood to deliver a toast to Sigyn and her children, Loki twitched his fingers and the wine turned to vinegar. The point was taken and Tyr did not rise again.

Vali and Narfi were mistrusted and disliked by the other Asgardians their age. More comfortable in the company of adults, they found most of the people their age shallow and gullible. They found it too easy to deceive them and constantly played jokes on them.

Being identical twins made the jokes all the easier to carry out. Now they were more or less shunned and chose to roam the castle and grounds to amuse themselves alone. It was during one of those excursions when they found the Room of Artifacts and the Casket of Jotunheim. As they grasped its handles, a blue tinge crept up their arms, into their faces. Shocked, they dropped the object onto its stand and rushed back into the upper levels of the Castle. Neither had chosen to speak of it since.

*　*　*

The weather was cold but clear and Vali wanted to take their horses for a ride into the nearby forest. Narfi was not so enamored with Mother Nature as Vali, but agreed to go. Vali chose to mount the large red stallion named Gilvar. Narfi rode a sleek black mare he nick named Crat, partly because of her real name, Cerrivat, and because it sounded like "cat" which seemed more suiting to her personality. They raced along the plains that lay in front of the forest. Crat, though smaller than Vali's big stallion, was swifter and Narfi reached the wood first. In spite of his initial reluctance, Narfi was now enjoying himself thoroughly and sat grinning as his brother caught up.

"Come on, slow poke, must you take all day?" teased Narfi as his brother cantered up beside him.

"Don't be silly, brother. I was holding back. If Gilvar ran full speed by that cat of yours, he would have knocked her to the ground," laughed Vali.

"Ha, and Mother said you had no imagination," said Narfi. With that, he turned and galloped into the forest.

Vali drew up beside him and they slowed their pace to a walk as the trees thickened. It was midday but the thick layer of branches and leaves overhead gave the forest the look of twilight. "I believe there are caves near here. Mother said that she, Father, and Thor would hide in them. Some are supposed to contain rare gems and gold," said Vali.

"What do you need of gems and gold?" asked Narfi. "Would you buy yourself your own kingdom, brother?"

Vali dismounted and led his horse to a small mound of earth just through a clump of bright green bushes. Under his breath he said, "Perhaps I would buy myself a new brother," and smiled at his own jest.

"A new brother? Not a bad idea, but I think I should like a sister this time," quipped Narfi as he, too, dismounted. The two exchanged shoves until they fell to the ground laughing. Vali stood up and began to circle the mound until he found what appeared to be an entrance. The opening was just big enough for the slender boys to crawl through, but they hesitated. The air coming from the opening smelled dank and uninviting. They dug away some dirt and carried off some rocks until the opening was wider and allowed for a little more light to enter the chamber. They could see that there was a sharp decline of earth leading down into what appeared to be an open cell of some kind. "Okay, brother, after you," offered Narfi.

Vali stared back at Narfi incredulously, one brow lifted. Then with a deep sigh, he jumped feet first into the opening. He slid down to the floor of the cave and looked about him. The light was too dim to see much of anything, so he conjured a cold, blue flame in the palm of his right hand. Now illuminated, the cave revealed delicate drawings of animals and crude figures carrying spears on its walls.

Narfi called from above. "What's it like? Are you alright? Is it safe?"

"Of course it's safe. What did you expect? Frost Giants?" laughed Vali.

"No, something more probable, like bears or wolves or something," replied Narfi. "You needn't be such an ass, you know."

"Oh, get over yourself, brother. Come on. It goes deeper," encouraged Vali.

Narfi slid awkwardly down the slope into the cave. He then conjured a cat made entirely of bright white light. It lit up the whole cell and some thirty feet into the cave. Vali extinguished his flame and shook his head with a smile, admiring once again his brother's greater finesse with his magical talent. Narfi waved his hand and the cat moved forward. Its strange, bright light lit up shiny minerals and bits of quartz in the cavern walls, making the cave sparkle before them. The cavern was tall and wide and they walked unimpeded for hundreds of feet. With the dropping of his hand, Narfi's cat came to a stop. Narfi signaled for his brother to stop, too. "Feel that?" he asked.

Vali stood stock still, and thought he felt a slight breeze on the left side of his face. "Yes, it's like air moving from over there." He indicated the wall to their left. Cautiously, he approached the solid rock, outstretching a hand slowly towards its surface. He leaned into it and sniffed. "Yes, there's air here, and it smells fresh. There must be a crack or something," he said, as he searched the rock. He went to touch the cave wall's rough surface only to have his hand pass through. He pulled it back. "Well, I certainly didn't expect that to happen."

Narfi pulled his brother away. "That can't be good," he began. "Portals like that, they don't usually lead to anywhere good." He looked back down the corridor they had just traversed. "We should go."

Vali leaned into the wall once more, smiling wickedly at Narfi's obvious discomfort. "Don't be silly, brother. I said the air smelled fresh. It's probably just a short cut Father invented years ago to hide from Thor. I'll bet it takes us back to the cave's entrance. Be brave, Narfi! Where's your spirit of adventure?"

"Spirit of adventure? I believe I left it down with that casket where we turned blue. No, Vali, leave it. If you really think Father had something to do with it, we should ask him. But we should not go through that portal!" Narfi reached for his brother's arm, but missed. With a wide grin, Vali vanished through the rock. Narfi groaned and stared at the spot where his brother had just been standing, hoping he would reappear just as suddenly. "Vali?" he called. "Vali, this isn't funny anymore. Come back, *now*!" Still, no Vali. With trembling hand, Narfi reached out to touch the rock and felt its solid surface. "Vali! Where are you?" he shouted. He ran his hands across more of the rock's face but found no portal.

Narfi thought he could hear the pounding of his heart echoing throughout the cave when a hand cupped his shoulder. With a yell, he turned and struck out at the one that had touched him. His brother, Vali, cried out with a yell of his own.

"By the gods, Narfi, I think you broke my nose!" shouted Vali, hands covering his face.

"Serves you right! Where were you? Didn't you hear me call for you? Where did you go?" demanded Narfi.

Vali thought a moment. "I really don't know. It was like a big, circular room, full of doors. Something told me to try the one I did and well, here I am. We should go back and try some of the other doors," he said.

"We can't," said Narfi. "The rock is solid now. I tried to go look for you, but there was no portal."

Vali touched the rock and his hand sank into it. "Well, it's back now. Maybe, while you're in the room, the door here closes until you go through another door. It's very strange magic indeed, but perhaps you're right. We should ask Father."

Narfi looked relieved. "That's a wonderful idea. Now, let's get out of here, okay? Too much weirdness for one day," he remarked.

CHAPTER 2

The boys returned to the Castle and found Thor presiding over the Counsel, their father, Loki, at the King's right hand side. Lavish golden benches lined the walls of the Great Entrance. Narfi lay face down on one, tracing the runes embedded into the tiles beneath him. Vali lay crossways, his head hanging off the front of the bench while his crossed legs stuck straight up into the air, a heel resting against the alabaster wall. Loki was slouched in his chair with one leg perched across the other knee, and seemed to be studying the stitching of his boot. He threw his head back in a great yawn and let his eyes wander around the room. He smiled as he spotted his sons resting opposite him. He jostled his brother, Thor, who had begun to snore softly, and whispered into his ear. Thor quickly glanced up at the twins and grinned. He nodded to Loki, who stood up quietly and left the table. The speaker continued nonstop to speak of the urgent need for a monument for some citizen or other neither of them had ever heard of.

Loki gathered up his sons and the three of them walked out to the expansive green lawns and gardens that overlooked the River of Asgard. They chose a soft spot in the warm sun not far from the river's edge. "Your mother and I used to sit here," Loki began. "As a matter of fact, it's where we..." he stopped himself, smiling. "That is, we had many a picnic here. But tell me, what is so important that you call away the King's First Counsel during important matters of State?" he asked, his face grave.

"Yes, we heard," said Vali. "A monument to Fredrik the Flatulent, was it?"

"Oh, no, Vali, it was the dedication of a park to Braki the Bilious," responded Narfi.

"Come now, boys. Surely you remember the famous Oliver the Odorous, whose great stench did drive the Frost Giants back to Jotunheim? A little respect, please," laughed Loki.

"Father, you once said that there were caves in the woods, and that you used to hide in them when you were young, like us." Vali felt unsure of how his father would react when he told him he had deliberately stepped through an uncharted portal.

"Yes, we did a lot of foolish things when we were young," said Loki, eyebrow raised in a wry smile.

Vali looked to his brother for help. Rolling his eyes, Narfi added, "We found a small opening that led to a large cavern amidst some green bushes near the edge of the Forest. There were cave drawings, and some crystals, and quartz." Narfi gauged the look on his father's face, and felt it safe to continue. "I conjured a cat made of light to guide us, so we went deeper into the cavern, and the path sloped down very gradually, and the path was wide, and the ceiling tall. We were never in any danger, really, Dad," Narfi concluded, words rushing. Loki didn't look convinced.

"So anyway," said Vali, "we started to feel this air sort of coming from the rock, but the rock wasn't really rock. I mean, you could walk right through it, so I did," he said nervously. "I mean, I figured it had to be something you left there, didn't you, Father?"

Loki remained thoughtful for a moment. "I've played a lot of tricks on the people of Asgard in my lifetime. As a result, every time anything unpleasant or inconvenient happens, everyone's first reaction is to assume that I am in some way responsible. I am not responsible for all the chaos in all the nine realms, and likewise, I am not responsible for all the magical phenomena that occur. I left no open portal in any cave, Vali. You're lucky you didn't get stuck in the stone, or meet some dark force when you stepped through that rock. No more visits to this cave. Portals like that usually lead nowhere good, understand?" Loki smiled. "I lost you both once. I don't want to ever lose you again," he added.

Vali studied his feet for a bit and then gave his father an almost imperceptible nod. Narfi felt bad for his brother, even though he had felt exactly the same as his father about passing through that cave wall.

"Father," Narfi began. "There was a room on the other side. Vali described it as a circular room filled with doors. He said something told him to pick the door he did, and when he went through it, he returned to the cave with me. He could have gone back to try more doors, but told me he wanted to talk to you first. Have you ever heard of such a room?"

Loki sighed, looking sideways at his sons. "You're not going to let this thing go, are you?" he asked.

The boys glanced at one another, and smiled guiltily. "No, Father, we're not," replied Narfi. "Neither would you, if you had found it." Narfi stood up straight, looking down at his father.

Loki got up. He still stood about half a foot taller than the twins and stared down at Narfi. "It has always been my contention that it is better to deceive than be deceived. It is my policy to avoid places with which I am unfamiliar. If I had come upon this portal deep in some cave," he paused, and broke into a smile, "I would have convinced my brother to go through first." He turned and started back towards the Castle, his back to the twins. "I don't want to hear that you two have been exploring any portals in any cave," he added, smiling to himself. He had chosen his words carefully. Although he worried about his sons' innate curiosity and the possible dangers they faced, he also knew who they were--Loki's sons, and they were not to be stopped.

Narfi and Vali exchanged looks. They understood their father perfectly. Narfi groaned inwardly with his knowledge of the inevitable. Vali grinned from ear to ear. "And so the adventure begins," he whispered to Narfi.

"Yes, I suppose it does," Narfi answered, much less enthusiastically.

Sunset was not far off, so Narfi convinced his brother to wait until morning to get back to the cave. They slept little, talking about their plans for the next day. "Vali, Father said we shouldn't go," reminded Narfi.

"No, he said only that he didn't want to hear of it. You know Father. You know what he meant. He's given us permission, Narfi, in his way," said Vali.

Narfi knew his brother was right but remained cautious. Vali had always been the hastier of the two. Narfi was conflicted; he admired his brother's courage but feared his desire to jump into harm's way. But then, he was curious, too. "We'll go shielded and invisible. Father's right. There could be danger."

Vali rolled his eyes. "Of course, brother, as you wish. But I assure you, there's nothing dangerous in that room. Just a lot of doors."

Narfi shook his head. "Still, my brother, we should be careful. I have no desire to die tomorrow."

Vali let out a laugh. "Must you always be so grim?" he asked. "I have no wish to die, either! We shall be shielded, and invisible...What could go wrong?"

Narfi sighed. It was all those possibilities he wished not to think about. So he put the thoughts of the dangerous consequences for what they were about to do out of his mind and tried to be as enthusiastic as his brother about the next day's adventure. "Right. What could go wrong? We are the sons of the god of Chaos. We are Loki's sons! We should be able to face any contingency and return triumphant! Loki's sons!" he concluded, with a shout.

"Loki's sons!" Vali shouted in reply.

CHAPTER 3

The boys awoke to the sound of thunder and the flash of lightening. Their first thought was that Thor must be displeased with something but sometimes, weather just happened. Narfi didn't take much stock in signs and portents, but the raging storm left him feeling uneasy about their plans to embark on a new adventure. The boys joined the others at breakfast but remained silent, each lost in his own thoughts.

Sigyn noticed the unusual quiet from her normally gregarious sons and remarked on it. "Didn't you sleep well?" she asked them.

Vali looked up with a jerk. "What? Oh, no, it's just that, well, we wanted to ride again today, but the storm..." His voice trailed off.

"It's just a summer storm," Sigyn said. "It should pass quickly. You should take your cousin, Jorda, with you. She's visiting here for a while, and since she knows no one in Asgard, I think you should befriend her and show her around."

The boys exchanged glances. Their mother had just thrown a huge cog into the wheels of their plans. They looked at their father, who had a mischievous smile on his face. "Yes. Nice girl. A bit younger than you, but you should all get along very well." Loki stole a knowing glance at his wife. Playing hosts to their cousin should keep them out of trouble. "You must make her feel welcome here. No tricks, understand?" he added.

Both boys groaned. "But Dad," Vali began. "Must we? I mean, a girl?" Disappointment showed on his face.

Narfi grabbed his brother's arm to silence him. "Of course, Mother, Father. It will be fun. We should have her meet us at the stables." Narfi, as always, had a plan.

As Sigyn had predicted, the storm dissipated by the time the boys reached the stables. They saddled their horses and waited impatiently for their new burden, their cousin Jorda. Narfi had asked the grooms to fetch and prepare Skaldra, one of the most unpredictable mares of the stables. Narfi assured the grooms that Jorda was an excellent rider and preferred a challenge. Before long, a tall, golden haired young woman strode into the open path between the stalls. The boys stood transfixed. They had expected a child, but this girl couldn't have been much younger than themselves. They stared open mouthed at probably the most beautiful girl they had ever seen.

"Is this my mount?" asked the girl, pointing to the nervous Skaldra.

With a start, Vali answered, "Y -yes..." he gulped, and then regained his composure. "Her name is Skaldra. Perhaps we should find another. Skaldra is a bit, well..." he stopped, glancing in his brother's direction.

Narfi closed his jaws with an audible snap as he looked back at Vali. 'Dear Father, god of Chaos,' he thought to himself. He extended his hand. "I'm Narfi," he introduced. "This is my brother, Vali. You must be Jorda. Mother suggested we show you around. We've planned to go riding, but my brother's right. You may wish to find a more," he paused, "gentle horse to ride."

Jorda approached the stomping Skaldra and stroked her nose. The horse immediately calmed and allowed Jorda to climb into the saddle without the slightest hitch. "This horse is fine. Shall we go?" she asked, her voice flat.

The boys mounted their own horses and the three of them set out across the vast fields that led to the forest. The twins gave each other a smiling glance and took off, passing Jorda as fast as their horses could carry them.

Jorda gave a sigh and shook her head. "Boys," she whispered to herself. Then she bent her head close to the horse's ear and whispered into it. Skaldra responded immediately, flew to catch up, and then pass, the racing twins. She pulled up short at the entrance to the forest, a sight sneer on her face. They brought their horses next to hers, laughing at their defeat.

"You're quite a rider," remarked Vali.

"I have a way with animals," she answered, her head held high, a look of satisfaction on her face. She could see that the boys were interested in her. Most boys were. She, in turn, had little interest in them. She much preferred the company of animals to that of any person, royal heritage or not. "Look," she continued. "You don't have to 'show me around.' I don't plan to be here very long. As a matter of fact, I hope to leave today. So, if you don't mind, I think I'll just go back to the Castle."

"No!" said Vali. "That is, we've found this most amazing cave, with a portal that leads who-knows-where. Come and explore with us," he pleaded.

Narfi stared at his brother in shock. Vali had just revealed their plans to this stranger who owed them no allegiance whatever and, from all appearances, didn't even like them. Narfi was sure she would ride back to the Castle and inform on them. Now committed, he had to find a way to convince this girl to participate in this reckless plan to prevent their discovery. "There are drawings," he offered. "Of animals, in the cave," he added. He knew at once that he had the girl's attention.

"Really?" she answered. "Cave drawings?" She pondered this information for a bit. "Perhaps I will go with you, to see the drawings," she suggested. "I should like to see what animals may have roamed these parts millenia ago. Lead the way," she commanded.

Vali was thrilled that Jorda was going to continue on with them, but Narfi was not. He found Jorda to be arrogant and cold. His persuasion of Jorda to join them was only to protect himself and his brother; he did not care for this new cousin of theirs. With a look of disgust, he followed behind the two as they entered the forest.

Vali found the cave entrance easily and hopped down from Gilvar. Narfi watched as Jorda slid down from Skaldra, and then he dismounted Crat. Vali jumped down into the cavern first, lighting the way for the others. Narfi gallantly bowed for Jorda to enter next, offering his hand in assistance. She ignored it and jumped in unaided. Narfi took a deep breath to quell the anger growing within him and followed the others down. Once in the cave, he conjured his cat again, filling the room with its bright light. He saw Jorda smile slightly at his choice of vessel for the illumination.

Jorda surveyed the room, lightly touching the drawings of the ancient beasts and people carefully painted on its walls. She was fascinated, finding the simple shapes extraordinarily beautiful. "They're wonderful," she whispered. There was warmth in her voice that did not go unnoticed by Narfi. He then caught sight of his brother, who was obviously infatuated with the girl. Narfi felt a strange stirring in his breast of, what? Envy? He scoffed, reminding himself that he detested this girl and remembered that she said she was leaving that day, anyway. He had always admired his brother's strength, but he had strengths of his own and had never been envious. He didn't like this feeling and did what he could to bury it.

Vali stood next to Jorda and pointed to a section of the wall depicting a herd of wild horses. The images showed a grace and elegance that he hadn't noticed before. This girl was going to be a good influence on him, he was sure. Vali was beginning to really see the beauty of this otherwise stark and barren cavern. He moved closer to her side. To his delight, she did not move away and she even smiled at him. Tentatively, he placed a hand gently on her back as they leaned closer to the drawings. She did not rebuff his touch. Vali was beside himself with joy.

Narfi cleared his throat. "Well, I suppose we should move on, you know, towards the portal. I mean, that is why we're here, is it not, brother?" he insisted, a slight edge to his voice.

"Oh," started Vali, dropping his hand. "Yes! Please, Jorda, come with us. You must see this," he insisted.

Jorda looked at Narfi, noticing the obvious irritation in his face. "Yes, I think I should like that," she answered with a mocking smile in Narfi's direction. With that, she took Vali's arm, and the two strode off in the direction of the portal the boys had discovered the day before. Narfi readjusted his feelings towards his cousin. He no longer disliked her. He hated her. He vowed to slit her throat if she did anything to hurt his brother. Vali's heart was so open and vulnerable. Narfi had veiled his own with a coat of ice the moment his own grandfather had banished them all to Siberia.

"Splendid," he remarked, his voice dripping with sarcasm as he followed them deeper into the cave.

As they approached the spot, Narfi called out to Vali, "Don't forget your shield," he said, feeling the warmth of his own protective bubble surround him.

Vali closed his eyes, conjured his own shield, and opened his eyes to see Jorda staring curiously at him. "It's a bit of magic we learned a long time ago," he assured her. Her face was still puzzled, so he continued. "You know that we're sorcerers, of course. Like our Dad, you know?"

Jorda was taken aback for just a moment, and then answered, "Oh, yes, of course," and smiled back at him.

Narfi turned away from the smiling couple and gestured, putting a finger down his throat. He then turned back. "Oh, dear, Jorda can't conjure up a shield. I guess she shouldn't go with us, then. Surely, you wouldn't want anything to happen to her, would you, brother?" Narfi smiled sweetly at Vali, who seemed unperturbed.

"No problem," Vali stated as he took Jorda's hand. She felt the warmth of the shield surround her, and smiled up at him, a sense of wonderment on her face.

Narfi grimaced slightly and sighed deeply. "Wonderful," he stated flatly. He placed a hand on Vali's shoulder. "When you went in before," he said, "the portal closed behind you. I think we should step in connected, all at once."

"Well, duh," responded Vali.

Narfi gritted his teeth. "What am I doing?" he asked himself. He never even wanted to come back here, and now he had to endure this humiliation by his own brother. It was all he could do not to blast Vali back to the entrance of the cave, but he controlled himself. He knew that Vali only wanted to impress this girl, but he really didn't like that it was to be at his own expense. Narfi gave his brother a shove and the three entered the circular chamber.

The chamber's only light came from the glowing outlines of the individual doors. The three of them turned in circles, examining each door. Narfi spoke first. "Okay, brother, which door leads out?" he asked.

Vali turned and turned again, but felt nothing. Nothing told him that this or that door led to the way out. "I don't know," he answered. "Before, I could sense where you were. Now, there's nothing. Didn't you notice which door we came through?"

"We didn't exactly come through any door, brother. We just sort of appeared here. Are you telling me you have no idea which door leads home?" Narfi's voice became harsh with anger.

"The idea of coming here wasn't so we could just turn around and go back. Just choose a door, and let's enter it. We'll mark each one we try until we find the one that leads back into the cave. Simple enough?" asked Vali, palms turned upward.

"You stupid idiot! What if the first door leads us into Jotunheim or into the bowels of Hela's realm itself? You said you sensed the correct door. Why can't you sense it now?" Narfi felt himself sliding into a rage.

Vali's face hardened. "I suppose I was sensing the presence of my brother, Narfi. You're the huge intellect here, Father's favorite…" He was unable to finish his sentence. Narfi had thrown himself at him, fists ready.

Vali shot a blast of power at his brother, sending him flying across the room. He stalked towards Narfi, arms outstretched, hands clawed, ready to blast again. Jorda ran between them, screaming, "Enough!" Vali lowered his arms, while Narfi remained seated on the chamber floor. The two brothers glared at one another but made no more moves to strike. Jorda paced between them, her hands covering her face. She muttered to herself, something about "not happening again."

Narfi picked himself up from the floor. Keeping his distance from his brother, he neared one of the doors. He placed his hands flat against it, and pressed an ear to it. He thought he heard something from it, a sort of low, drubbing noise thrummed behind it. "This one sounds safe. Sort of," he ventured. "At least, I don't hear any screaming giants or howling wolves."

Jorda whirled on Narfi, shouting, "What do have against wolves? What have they ever done to you?" Vali looked at her in alarm. She seemed to be losing control. First, mumbling to herself, and now, screaming about the poor wolves. He tried to take her hands away from her face. She resisted a little, and then, resignedly, let him wipe away her tears.

As Narfi watched, he felt the anger within him beginning to subside.

"There's something I should tell you," Jorda began. She wrung her hands and began pacing again. "I'm the daughter of the goddess Jord, the goddess of primitive things--animals, primal emotions, all that. Sometimes I forget the effect I have on people. It's my fault that you turned on each other. Mother thought that if I left Alfheim for a while, the effect might wear off. Obviously, it hasn't." She hung her head and crossed her arms.

Vali and Narfi looked at each other and began to laugh. "So, your power is your enormous ability to piss people off?" asked Narfi through the laughter.

Jorda looked up sharply, then cracked a smile, and began to laugh as well. Somehow, the spell had been broken. She had been angry with both of them when they had set out from the stables. She had been angry with everyone at Asgard. Her feelings had changed abruptly when she saw the two brothers attack one another. She had a sudden revelation. She must control her own emotions if she was to prevent such outbursts of emotion from others. Feeling a wave of new calmness, she replied, "Yes, I suppose it is." She walked to the door in front of which Narfi was standing. "This one?" she asked.

Vali approached them and pressed his own ear to the door. "It's strange, like some sort of machinery or something."

"Shall we give it a try?" asked Narfi.

"May as well," said Vali. "We've got to start somewhere." He took his dagger from its sheath, and scored a large "X" across the door. "After you, brother," Vali said, bowing low to Narfi.

Narfi responded with a disdainful look at Vali, but cautiously began to pull the door open just slightly. He took a tentative peek through the crack he had made. He saw a flat, wet surface in front of him. Beyond that was a white railing of some sort, and beyond that, the sea. "It seems to be a ship," he whispered. "It looks deserted. Follow me," he signaled, and the three walked on board. Vali allowed the door to shut behind Jorda and then opened it quickly again. In place of the room of doors in front of him, he was staring at what appeared to be a broom closet. He tapped Narfi on the shoulder, nodding his head towards the closet. Narfi's face went white.

"Don't panic," he said. "Don't panic. It'll be Okay. J-j-just don't panic," Narfi repeated. He felt himself start to hyperventilate.

Vali pushed Narfi's head down, gently. "That's it, brother. Take some deep breaths. Keep the head down. That's it," he urged, taking a few deep breaths of his own.

Jorda crept silently out onto the deck, looking for any signs of life. She was wearing her summer riding clothes, consisting of a sleeveless leather vest, leather shorts, and tall leather riding boots. The frigid ocean wind stung her arms and thighs. By law, the boys were required to wear the symbols and markings appropriate for their royal station, which meant they wore sleeves over their arms, long pants, and boots. Since it was summer the material was thinner, and they, too, shivered in the frigid North Sea wind. Vali spied a blanket left draped across a deck chair and placed it around Jorda's shoulders. The deck looked deserted, so they began walking aft, hoping to find a door into someplace warm. About halfway down the long deck, they found what they were seeking. Peering inside, they discovered an open and empty room. It must have belonged to someone of privilege, judging from its size and lavish furnishings. There were several trunks covered with various pieces of clothing. Other clothing was strewn across the floor.

They recognized the style of clothing to be those of the humans of Earth. This was actually good news to Vali and Narfi, since they had been taught how to travel from earth to Asgard by their teacher, Syr. Quickly, they donned what they took to be evening clothes. Jorda took some gowns into the room's bath and emerged, looking every bit the daughter of a goddess. She was more accustomed to leather that to lace, but she rather enjoyed flaring the long chiffon skirts about her. She pulled a heavy woolen cape trimmed in ermine around her. The three, satisfied they would probably blend in if caught, left the room to look for signs of a hidden portal. As they came closer to the rear of the ship, they heard the sounds of music and laughter. They looked through a window and saw a large ballroom full of humans, some dancing, some drinking and laughing. There against a wall stretching almost the whole width of the ballroom stood a table covered in food. Vali nudged Narfi to take a look and they both stared longingly at the various dishes laid out upon it.

"I'm hungry, too," said Jorda. "Let's go in."

Narfi turned to face her. "I dunno," he hesitated. "It might be too risky to…" He was interrupted as his brother brushed by him on the way into the ballroom. Jorda gave Narfi a little smile and a wave and walked into the room behind Vali. Narfi dropped his head in resignation and reluctantly walked in behind them. They joined a handful of other guests as they filled their plates with sliced meats, salads, and desserts. A couple sitting at a large table near the band invited them to sit. Thankful, they joined the little group and dove hungrily into their dinner. The conversations around them indicated that this was the ship's maiden voyage. The couple with them went on about the beautiful Grand Staircase, the wonderful food, and the luxurious appointments in the state rooms. They confided that this trip constituted their honeymoon, having left Southampton, England four days earlier, on April tenth.

Narfi idly fingered the menu that lay on the white linen covered table. "RMS Titanic," it read. April fourteenth. RMS Titanic. Some memory stirred in his mind. Something he had read about Earth's history. "Excuse me," he asked the young woman seated nearest him. "What year is this?" She eyed him suspiciously. "Please, I, I, uh, I'm from France."

The woman gave a little laugh and said, "It's 1912, silly. Are the years counted differently in France?"

Narfi shot out of his chair. "Vali! Jorda! We have got to get out of here, *now*!" he shouted. The two looked at him as though he had gone mad. "No, really. This is not a good place to be. Vali, this is the Titanic! Remember? Iceberg? Many lives lost? Mother told us about it. She said some people liked to blame Dad for it."

Vali's eyes widened. "By the gods! How the hell did we wind up here? Quick, Jorda, we've got to get back on deck and find north. What time is it?" Vali asked a man sitting nearby.

The man pulled a gold watch from his vest pocket. "11:37, according to this," he reported.

"Minutes!" yelled Narfi. "It hits the iceberg at 11:40! *Run!*" he urged.

The three rushed out onto the deck. They scoured the night sky till they spotted the North Star. Just then, there was a horrible sound of screaming metal as the ship was violently torn by the huge underwater iceberg. Everyone was thrown forward as the great ship dragged itself along the killer ice. They scrambled back onto their feet, arms locked together, a twin on either side of Jorda. They turned their faces to the North Star and a swift moment after closing their eyes, the twins and Jorda transported off the fated ship. They opened their eyes again, expecting to find themselves back safely on the Rainbow Bridge. Instead, they arrived back in the chamber of doors. They stared at one another in stunned silence. After a few moments, Vali spoke. "Well, that's one door down."

CHAPTER 4

Narfi and Jorda looked at Vali as if he had gone totally insane. Then they looked at each other, and the absurdity of it all came to them. They laughed softly at their hopeless situation. "At least we got something to eat," reminded Jorda. They chuckled a bit at this and proceeded to sit on the floor, backs against the wall. "So, there are, seven, eight, nine of them all together. Eight more doors, unless we get lucky sooner. Who chooses next?" Jorda asked.

"I will," stated Vali. He stood up and began to circle the room, holding his hands, fingers spread, close to their surfaces. He slowed down at one in particular and said, "This one feels warm. Better clime, maybe?" he suggested. He scored an "X" on its surface and opened the door. He smiled as he gazed into what looked like a cavern. "Here we are. Home again." He held the door for the others, pleased with himself as they filed out.

"No, Vali," differed Narfi as he looked around him. "This isn't home. This looks a lot like…" he stopped, as the sound of muffled screams and cries of pain and anguish rose from deep beneath their feet. "Helheim," he concluded.

"Helheim?" exclaimed Jorda. "You've sent us to Hell, Vali?"

"You've got to admit, from here, it looks like any other cave, doesn't it?" Vali tried to sound indifferent.

Narfi shook his head. "There's no transporting out of here, brother. Hela has seen to that. We have no powers here at all." Even though the temperature was overly warm here, he clutched his jacket close. They had heard stories that Hela was a vampire, or a cannibal, a werewolf, or a poisonous snake. There were no legends suggesting she was a fluffy kitten or a plump old grandmother baking cookies. A sinister hissing sound began to rise from the depths.

The three clumped closely together, the boys trying gallantly to shield Jorda. A hazy green light hung about a dozen yards ahead of them. The light steadily grew less hazy, shaping itself into the form of a person. The shape became more distinct and it was obviously a woman. She was clearly in focus now, her face so beautiful, it was almost painful to look at. Jorda looked away, but the boys couldn't force their eyes off of her. Her dress was of a material so sheer as to be almost nonexistent. Her beauty was unparalleled, until one got to see below her waist. At her waistline, her skin became dark. Patches of skin and muscle had rotted away, and as one looked below her knees, all one saw were bones left bare. She spoke, her voice a deep, gravelly whisper.

"A visit from the sons of Loki," she remarked. "Fancy meeting you here," she added.

Narfi spoke with some trepidation. "Y…yes, we hadn't expected to meet you, either, Lady Hela, at least, not so soon. We've run into a sort of problem. Hope maybe you can help?" He peered anxiously into Hela's face. He thought he detected signs of interest, so he went on. "You see, we sort of wandered into this room, and it looks like we can't find the right door to get out. Have you ever heard of such magic?" He looked at her hopefully.

She stared at the boys, studying their faces. At last, she addressed them again. "You have nothing to fear from me," she said. "I would no more kill you than harm my own…"she paused, smiling. "…Brothers." She glided closer. "If I should decide to help you, what's in it for me?" she asked, just inches from Narfi's face.

Hela's voice stank of death and decay. Narfi did his best not to look revolted and, at the same time, tried to come up with a suitable answer. Tentatively, he asked, "What would you like, My Lady?"

Hela smiled at his answer. She knew they had nothing to offer. She also knew that she could not keep them here; it was not their time. The presence of these vital, young people, however, refreshed her, and she wanted to keep them with her as long as possible. She drifted over to Jorda. "Give me your friend, here. Give me your friend in exchange for your freedom," she purred to Narfi, as she stroked Jorda's face.

The point where Hela's finger touched Jorda's skin left a dark red mark. Vali stepped forward. "No. That will not do. We won't leave without her," he insisted, his face red with anger.

Hela glided to within inches of Vali's face now. Vali made no pretense of his revulsion, gagging as she breathed on him. "So brave, to give up your life and the life of your brother to save this…" She paused, looking at Jorda. "…Girl." She backed away towards the rear of the cavern. "My bargain is this," she said, "I demand a day of each of your lives. One day each year."

The trio thought this over. "That doesn't sound so bad," said Vali.

"No, it sounds reasonable to me," added Jorda.

Narfi was more thoughtful. "I guess it depends on the day," he wondered. "I mean, it could be inconvenient…"

"Inconvenient?" Vali's voice was full of surprise. "What can be more inconvenient than death, my brother? We should take the deal, unless you can come up with a better way to escape Hell."

Narfi responded to Hela's demand. "We would give you a day, My Lady, but are we permitted to choose which day? That is, we should like to inform our families, so that they might not worry about our disappearances," he said.

Hela laughed at this response. Then, she began to grow until her presence filled the cave. "You would *dare* to place conditions on me? You weak, little person! I am Hela, and I could devour you whole!"

The three shrank back. Vali punched his brother's shoulder. "Now you've gone and done it," he said reproachfully.

Narfi flinched, sweat beginning to break out on his brow. "Seemed a reasonable request, at the time," he responded meekly, rubbing his arm.

"Silence!" roared Hela. She shrank back to her original form and then addressed them once more. "I'll give you a date to prepare for each year. You will attend me on your birthdays. At sunrise, you shall appear here, and at sunset, you will be returned to your homes." She appeared in front of Narfi's face once more, her smile wicked. "Does that suit you, little Asgardian?" she asked him.

Narfi opened his mouth to speak but shut it when his brother punched him again. "I was going to say," he began, shooting a stern look in Vali's direction, "that your demands are accepted. You have your day. Now, would you be so kind as to fulfill your part of the bargain?"

Hela chuckled. "You are very like your father, boy. He was never quick to seal a deal, either." She began to glow more brightly. "So be it. Your destination lies beyond this door." A doorway materialized in the cave wall to their left. "See you soon," she crooned, and then disappeared.

The three rushed through the doorway, disappointed to find they were back in the chamber of doors once more. Jorda looked around and moaned. "She lied to us."

Narfi looked at the ground and sighed. "No she didn't. All she said was that she would help us leave Helheim. We should have been more specific."

Vali patted his brother's back in encouragement. "At least we're out of there," he said. "And," he added, "who knows? An alliance with the Queen of the Dead might prove useful someday. Now Jorda, it's your turn to pick a door. Let's hope yours is less disastrous than either of ours."

Jorda walked around the room, touching each door in turn. She stopped and lingered at one, a smile easing the fear from her face. "This one," she said. "I feel something here, something familiar."

"This must be the door!" cried Vali. "She's the only one that has 'felt' something. She must be sensing it's the way home!" Vali rushed to Jorda's side and hugged her and then lowered his arms, his face flushing. "Oh, I'm sorry…I was just…"

"No, that was quite all right," smiled Jorda. She took his hand, and the two gazed at one another.

Narfi rolled his eyes, and said, "Shall we go now, or should I turn my back and give you two some privacy?"

Vali and Jorda blushed and then tried to compose themselves. "No, let's go," said Jorda.

As with the other doors, they marked this one and then Jorda led the way inside. The door opened onto a lush valley of the greenest grass and most beautiful flowering trees. Songbirds flew overhead, and a pond covered with pink and white water lilies rested nearby. Jorda took a deep breath and exclaimed, "This is Alfheim! My ties are with Alfheim, not Asgard, so the door led me here!" She danced about the meadow, arms flung wide. "Isn't it beautiful? Tell me it's beautiful!"

Vali and Narfi had no choice but to agree. This was indeed a world of incredible beauty. They watched Jorda as she plucked purple and yellow wildflowers near the pond's edge. She smiled up at them. Then her expression changed as she stared at something behind them, so the boys spun around to see for themselves. Six warrior Elves had managed to encircle them, spears pointed at their chests. The boys and Jorda raised their hands instinctively in submission, and were led away.

Jorda tried to appeal to them. "Wait, I am the daughter of Jord. We mean you no harm. This is my homeland. Please, just take me to my Mother. She can vouch for me."

The warriors ignored her, and Narfi whispered to Vali, "I've tried to disappear but cannot. It seems our magic is useless here."

Vali replied, "Yeah, I tried to raise my shield, but nothing happened. I suppose our magic worked only in Midgard because the Earth is so primitive and has so little magic of its own."

They marched for what felt like miles until they reached an elaborate tent, gilded and encrusted with jewels. They were escorted inside where they found Frey, the Vani god of fertility and former King of Vanaheim, sitting behind a vast, ornately carved desk. Frey continued to write on a piece of parchment, paying no heed to his new prisoners. At last, he put down his pen and faced the three young people standing tall in front of him. "What's this? The Aesir are sending children to fight their battles now?"

Vali spoke first. "Lord Frey, it is I, Vali. This is Narfi and Jorda. Surely you know us. What goes on here?"

Narfi spoke next. "You are at war with Asgard," he said, his tone matter of fact. "Of course you don't recognize us. We haven't been born yet," he added, looking at Vali and Jorda.

Frey studied the dark-haired boy and his identical brother. "You do look familiar. If I didn't know better, I'd say you look like that fox, Loki. But then, perhaps you are. Perhaps this is another of your tricks." He signaled for his guards. "Take these three and put them with the other prisoners of war!"

"Wait!" shouted Narfi. "If I was Loki, I could easily have vanished by now, could I not?" he struggled against the grip of the guards.

Frey considered this. "Yes, but you're clever, too." He eyed them for a few more moments. "Take them someplace underground, away from the others," he commanded. "Keep a close eye on them. I may find use for them yet." With that, they were marched away.

Sitting on the rough floor of their cell, which was lit only by one small torch, they tried to think of some way to escape. A rat crawled into the cell with them and Jorda placed it tenderly in her lap, stroking it gently. The boys made a face but did not try to deter her. Narfi's back straightened as an idea came to him. "Jorda, can you communicate with these animals?" he asked.

"Of course," she replied, "and they with me. What good is that? Shall I have the mice and rats overwhelm the guards and carry us off to safety?" She tried to sound sarcastic, scoffing at his insinuation.

"Something like that, yeah," he replied.

Vali understood exactly what his brother was suggesting. "Yes! But not mice and rats," he said. "Something bigger, maybe?" He looked at her, eyes hopeful.

Jorda shook her head. "No. I won't use them that way. Animals will not attack unless frightened or starving. I won't have them attack, even to save myself!"

Vali took her hand. "They don't have to attack," he said, assuring her. "They just need to scare some people."

She shook her head and wailed, "What if they did? What then? We'll still be stuck here in ancient Alfheim, enemies of the state!"

"One thing at a time," said Narfi. "First, we get out of this cell. Then, we escape from Alfheim. There must be Asgardians here. Spies, maybe. We'll find help and then we'll be able to leave."

"Please, Jorda," begged Vali. "You're our only hope."

Jorda looked at the earnestness in Vali's eyes and relented. She raised the rat to her face and whispered softly in its ear. With a gentle stroke, she set it down again on the ground and it scurried through the bars and down the darkened corridor. "Well," she said, "it's all up to Davli, now." She leaned against Vali's chest and sighed.

Hours passed. The trio slept. Vali and Narfi sat back to back, propping each other up, heads drooping in sleep. Jorda rested her head in Vali's lap. The sound of a loud crash down the corridor woke them. They jumped up and ran to the bars, straining to see what was happening. There was a scream and a roar, followed by what sounded like metal crashing to the floor. Heavy thuds could be heard approaching their cell. In the faint light, they beheld its source.

Narfi's and Vali's jaws dropped has they looked upon what had to be the largest bear they had ever seen. Jorda grinned as she reached her arms through the bars to scratch behind the huge beast's ears. It pushed its head against the cell door, and Jorda whispered to it in some unintelligible language that Narfi and Vali assumed was Bear Talk. The bear wrapped its enormous claws around the metal bars and pulled. With little effort, it ripped the entire front of the cell from the rock, and they were free.

Vali and Narfi eyed the bear with some apprehension, but Jorda assured them that so long as they were with her they would not be harmed. The giant bear greeted them with a loud roar and then lumbered down the corridor towards the exit. They ran from the cell and came to the opening of the cave. They found that night had fallen, giving them additional cover. The guards had fled and in their terror, had dropped their spears. Vali and Narfi each took one and they all surveyed the landscape. Vali whispered, "Frey mentioned other prisoners. Perhaps they can help us."

"I sensed that there was a veil near here," said Narfi. "It was just this feeling of magical deceit. You know the feeling, brother?" Narfi grinned.

"Oh, yes, brother, I know it well," answered Vali. Hunched low, the little party made its way down a low hill to a flattened area of grass about two hundred feet square. The boys felt a low hum of magical energy. "It's here," he informed Jorda, who kept close to his side.

Narfi reached out a hand and encountered a surface as hard as stone. "I don't think we can get through," he moaned.

"Come on, now, brother, there must be a way. Think!" Vali said encouragingly.

Narfi thought back to the teachings of Syr. She said magic was all about particles and charges. Just change the charges of the particles and one could manipulate anything.

He willed the charges of his hand and those of the barrier to change and tried again, but the wall remained solid. Obviously there was something here that was blocking his power. He tried to think again. He felt the heavy metal spear in his hand. Perhaps there was a way… "Vali," he whispered. "Hit my spear with yours."

Vali looked puzzled. "They'll hear us," he said.

"They might, but just strike it once. I believe the clash will cause a spark, and it might just short out this spell," he explained.

Vali grinned at his brother. "That's why I love you, brother. You're always the man with the plan." He swung his spear and with one loud crash, brought it down soundly against Narfi's spear. As predicted, there was a bright flash as the spears connected and the veil disappeared. There before them stood about fifty people, all staring in their direction. The hold was not guarded, so sure was Frey that the veil would keep anyone from aiding his prisoners to escape. Narfi heard one small voice from the group whisper, "Look! It's Loki!" They rushed over and surrounded the trio. "Not only one Loki. He's made himself a doppelganger!" said another.

Vali made to set them straight, but Narfi grabbed his arm before he could speak. "Yes, I'm here to rescue you. Unfortunately, cancelling this veil has left my powers temporarily weak. You must take us to the closest connection to the Bifrost, so we may return and recover," he told them.

The prisoners were a bit skeptical, but they were free after all and didn't question him further. The tallest man there, one called Kevirsen, agreed to show them the way. The entire group crept as silently as possible to a small clump of trees near Frey's headquarters. They came upon a circle marked with Asgardian runes in the center of the trees. They all packed themselves tightly within the circle, and Kevirsen called out, "Heimdall, take us back!" A cry rang out from Frey's tent. The group waited impatiently for Heimdall's response. Kevirsen called out again. "Heimdall! We need you to recall us *now*!" he thundered. A moment later, a brilliant light engulfed them all, and they were swept away.

Again, the three hoped against hope that they would find themselves on the Rainbow Bridge with the others, but it was not to be. They plopped down onto the floor of the chamber, faces in their hands. "It will be interesting to see," said Narfi, "if there are any tales of Father's brave rescue of the prisoners of Alfheim.

Vali smirked. "That's very doubtful, brother. More than likely, Kevirsen took the credit. Father himself probably denied it." Then he thought some more. "Well, maybe he didn't, at that." They laughed, but that died away as they pondered their next move.

"We've visited three doors and wound up in three realms," Narfi stated. "I'm beginning to wonder if it really matters which door we choose. I think we must face and triumph over disasters in each Realm before we will be allowed to return to Asgard. I think this place was conjured up by Odin to test his warriors."

"Or his sons," Vali added. "He knew Thor and Dad used to explore these caves all summer long. Perhaps he hoped they would find this portal and then overcome its obstacles and thus be proven worthy to be King."

"If that's the case," said Jorda, striding over to the next door, "then let's be at it. It would have been nice if our weapons remained with us instead of going on to Asgard with Kevirsen. Oh well, three down, six to go." She yanked open the door, which Vali hastily marked, and stepped through.

The world went completely white. The frigid air caught them and bent them over as they tried to avoid the blasts of arctic air. "This must be Niflheim," shouted Vali, trying to be heard over the wind.

"Can you see anything?" Narfi shouted back. "Can you see any sort of shelter?" He placed a hand above his eyes, trying to shade the blinding brightness of the snow covered landscape.

"Over here," Jorda yelled to them. "I think there's a cave here." She pulled Vali's arm, which he used to catch his brother, and the three trudged arm in arm through blowing snow towards what looked like a gray hole in the side of a mountain.

After a few moments, though it felt like hours, they were inside of a deep depression in the rock. The air still threatened to freeze them to the bone but they were out of the wind. Huddling together, they did what they could to warm themselves. "Niflheim. Hell's hell! At least there can't be any conflict here; Niflheim is conflict enough," groaned Narfi.

Vali rubbed Jorda's arms vigorously. "Be nice to have a bit of magic right now, wouldn't it?" he smiled. Jorda smiled wanly back at him and leaned into his chest.

"I would pick the worst possible realm of all," she replied. "How in the name of the gods are we going to get out of here?"

Narfi sat on the floor of the cave and drew his knees up to his chest. He wrapped his arms around his legs and laid his head down, trying hard to think. All the realms were connected by the World Tree Yggdrasil, so there had to be a way out. He looked around the cave, turned himself around, and stared towards the back. He decided to do a little exploring and forced himself to stand. As he neared the rear of the cave he could see that a passageway veered off it towards the left. "Here!" he called. "I think I may have found something!"

A crack hundreds of feet overhead allowed some daylight into the corridor. At one point, the passage opened up into a small room. A few large bones were scattered on the floor and a small heap of furs rested in a corner. They pounced on the furs, huddled closely together, and covered themselves warmly. Within a few minutes they had fallen asleep. After a few hours, Jorda woke with a start, wakening the other two as well. "Shh! I think I heard something," she whispered.

Vali and Narfi looked at each other with apprehension. "Strange noise in a strange land? That can't be good," whispered Vali.

"Maybe it's the people who left these furs," said Narfi. "Now they're coming back with some lovely soup and piles of roasted potatoes," he added, with a grin.

"And wonderful baked apples with honey and roast lamb with gallons of gravy!" added Vali.

"Stop!" said Jorda. "You're just making me hungrier! I'm about ready to start chewing on these furs, I'm so hungry!"

Their laughter died down as the realization of the hopelessness of their situation began to dawn on them. Vali raised his fist to his brother, who bumped it with his own. "We survived Siberia," said Vali.

Narfi let out a humorless snort. "This is not Siberia, brother. At least there, we had Mother and Syr. We had our magic. What have we here but a pile of moldy old furs? I haven't the slightest idea what to do. We are at the very bottom of Yggdrasil, even below Helheim. Won't Hela be disappointed when we miss our next birthday with her!"

Jorda's eyes widened. "What you just said, Narfi… We're at the bottom of Yggdrasil. I think we may find a way out!" Narfi just stared at her. "Just think, what lies at the very bottom of Yggdrasil?"

He pondered her question. "Nothing, except…" He began to understand. "Except for the beast, Nidhogg. The dragon chews at the roots of Yggdrasil, but what good is that? Would you have us die quickly, eaten by the serpent, rather than die slowly, freezing and starving to death?"

"No, think! If she chews on the root, then the root must be open. The veins of Yggdrasil feed all nine of the realms, feed the entire universe! If we can make our way to Nidhogg and elude her, we could enter the heart of Yggdrasil itself! As we know, Asgard is at its core. If we find the root, we find the way home!"

Narfi considered this plan. "Impossible," he concluded. "And this is exactly why we're going to try it!"

"Of course!" cried Vali. "This is precisely the sort of thing Loki's sons would do! Slay the dragon and ride the pulse of Yggdrasil back home!"

"Only one problem," said Narfi. "How are we going to find Nidhogg?"

Jorda smiled. "I have a way with animals," she said. With that, she closed her eyes, moving her head slightly from side to side as if listening. "She isn't far. If we can find a way down, I believe she lies directly beneath us."

They wrapped and tied as many furs as they could around them. Jorda said that besides giving them warmth, the furs would help to disguise their scent. Vali picked up what appeared to be a giant's thigh bone as a weapon. The three then began to search for a passage down and soon discovered the only way down was to leave the cave and climb down from the outside. Carefully, they made their way down, down, down. Jorda stopped them for a moment and listened. "That's not the wind," she said. She was talking about the loud hissing they heard rising up from beneath them.

They continued their descent until they saw a starry sky below them. They had reached the bottom of all the realms, the roots of Yggdrasil. Down was up, up was down. After a moment's disorientation, they righted themselves and the sky was again above them, and the ground was below them once more.

Jorda listened intently and then began to summon the dragon. A loud crunching sound signaled that Nidhogg had heard and was approaching. Vali tried to drag Jorda behind some snow covered rocks, but she shooed him off, eager for the dragon's appearance.

Then suddenly, Nidhogg was there. At first, it looked as though a piece of the mountain had broken away and fell towards them. Then they realized it was the head of Nidhogg--huge and white, spikes like rocky crags sticking out all over her head. Her eyes and tongue were blood red, all the more red compared to the whiteness of her skin. Jorda signaled the boys to hide, which they did reluctantly. The dragon spied Jorda, tongue flicking in and out between huge yellow-white teeth. She seemed unconcerned about Jorda's presence, and then suddenly reared her head as if to attack.

Vali jumped out from behind his rock long enough to grab Jorda and pull her to safety. The dragon struck, her razor sharp teeth biting through the snowy rocks where Jorda had once stood.

"Are you sure you can speak her language?" Vali asked. "Maybe you just insulted her mother or something."

"No, I can only speak the language of the one whom I address. As I do, the words sound to me as they would to you, but to the creature, they are heard in her language alone. I think she may be mad," Jorda said.

"So we're facing a dragon that's bigger than a mountain, and she's insane to boot? This is turning out to be a truly horrible day," said Narfi, mouth turned up in his father's crooked smile.

Vali took the large bone and broke it on his knee. "I have a plan," he announced. Before Narfi or Jorda could stop him, he ran out and jumped onto the serpent's nose. Startled, Nidhogg did not move quickly enough and Vali took each bone shard, sharp as knives at its broken ends, and rammed them into the beast's huge eyes. Nidhogg reared back in sudden surprise and pain. Vali jumped down and ran to the hiding place of Jorda and Narfi. Nidhogg reared, shaking her great head from side to side. She stretched her wings out full and began to rise. Blasts of wind from each beat of her wings hit them as they watched the beast fly off.

"We had better move quickly," Jorda urged. "She will probably return. Blinded, she will seek out familiar scents. All she has known for centuries is the root. It is home to her."

They scrambled as quickly as possible over snow covered rocks and rubble till they found pools of amber scattered amongst the rocks. Exploring further, they found open veins of sap oozing from the roots of Yggdrasil. Narfi continued to look, finding what looked like a small green tunnel that was making a soft sucking sound as it drank from melted snow. "I think I've found it!" he called to the others. "If we crawl in, the tree should take us back to Asgard," he told them, with some uncertainty in his voice.

"Can we breathe?" asked Vali, picturing the three of them trapped in a tube being slowly sucked upwards for miles.

Narfi put his hand on his brother's shoulder. "Do we have a choice?" he asked. "Die here at the hands of Nidhogg, or die trying to escape? At least this way, our bodies will make it back, and I for one, do not like the idea of being eaten alive."

Vali considered these options and then climbed next to a large tear in the root. The tree had a definite pulse as it took huge, sucking drafts of water and snow every few seconds. The sucking of water and nutrients was so strong that Vali felt his body rock to and away from it. "Alright, then, I'll go first, then you, Jorda, and you last, brother. Are we ready?" He took a deep breath to steady himself, waited for the next pause between beats, and lay down within the huge vein. Within seconds, there was a whooshing sound as Vali was carried away.

Narfi helped Jorda into the vein next and then waited as she, too, disappeared. Finally, he stepped into and lay down in the vein, closed his eyes, and felt himself carried rapidly up into Yggdrasil's great circulatory system.

Once inside the vein, they were in utter darkness. The only sound was the loud thrumming of Yggdrasil's heart as they sped up and up towards it. By holding their heads up, there was just enough room to breathe. The vein began to narrow as their pace quickened. The thrumming was incredibly loud now, and Vali and the others discovered it was more and more difficult to find air. Narfi felt that he might be crushed as the walls of the vein closed ever more tightly around him. He heard a small yelp from Jorda ahead of him and then, as he struggled to take another breath, he lost consciousness.

CHAPTER 5

Vali and Jorda stood over Narfi's prone body. "Is he breathing?" asked Jorda. "I don't think he's breathing," she said, her voice tight with fear.

Vali dropped down next to his brother, shaking him violently. "Narfi!" he shouted. "Narfi! Wake up! Narfi, please..." his voice trailed off.

With a sudden jolt and gasp of air, Narfi opened his eyes. He looked around and saw that they were back in the room of doors. He flopped onto his back, taking in great gulps of air, and then raised himself up on his elbows. "Well, that's something I wouldn't want to try again," he said, laughing.

The others joined him in the relieved laughter, knowing how closely they had escaped death.

"Seems unfair. All that, and here we are again, in this stupid, damned room," complained Jorda.

"Yes, but better here than in the belly of the beast," reminded Vali.

Narfi looked down at his clothes. "At least we're dry. So, we've conquered four of the nine realms. That only leaves five and one of those is Asgard. What have we left? We've been through Midgard, Alfheim, Helheim, and Niflheim."

"That leaves Muspellsheim, Vanaheim, Jotunheim, and Svartalfaheim. Not much to look forward to, is there?" asked Vali with a small chuckle. He reached down and helped his brother stand.

Narfi approached Jorda and held out his hand. "You were brilliant," he told her. "I'm sorry if I've been, well…" Words failed him.

Jorda took his hand. "No need to apologize, Narfi. It was my fault we got off to a bad start. I just wanted to be home with Mother, so I hated the both of you before I even met you. I let my emotions get the better of me and passed my resentment on to you. I would say we're even now." She smiled up at him.

Narfi dropped her hand and glanced at his brother. Vali was looking at his feet, avoiding the scene between Jorda and Narfi. "Okay, then. Are we ready to try another?" he asked.

Jorda groaned as she slumped resignedly back to Vali's side, slipping her hand into his. "Yes, I suppose we should. The sooner we go through them all, the sooner we return home, right?" she asked, looking into Vali's face.

"Right. At least that's what we're counting on. I think we should take…" Vali turned around, surveying the remaining doors. "This one," he concluded, pointing to an unmarked door.

"Alright, then. Let's have at it!" cheered Narfi, fist in the air.

"Ah, brother, your enthusiasm clearly masks the overwhelming fear that I know beats within your breast," laughed Vali.

"Never, my brother! I'm filled with the greatest anticipation!" He widened his eyes with an exaggerated look of abject fear, and then grinned.

The two bumped fists again and slapped one another's backs. Vali slashed an 'X' on the door, grabbed the handle, and pulled.

* * *

"Out of the ice and into the fire," mumbled Narfi, as they entered the fiery realm of Muspellsheim. The heat was intense and fires rose and crackled everywhere. A river of lava flowed in a deep valley in the distance. Directly ahead of them stood the enormous glowing throne of Surt, the god of Muspellsheim. Surt was a giant with flames for eyes, and fire seemed to glow behind numerous scars and cuts covering the warrior giant's body. Surt stood as he spied the intruders, and motioned for his guards to bring them closer.

Jorda gripped Vali's hand so tightly that he grimaced. "It'll be alright," he assured her, knowing full well he didn't have a clue what to do next. He glanced at Narfi, who let a wry smile cross his face.

"This doesn't promise to be a day any better than the last, does it?" Narfi asked.

The guards stood on either side of the little party and they were marched in front of Surt. Surt stared down at them, face stern. "What brings you here, little Asgardians?" he demanded. "Have you come to return what was stolen from me?"

They looked at one another, faces puzzled. "I am sorry, my lord, of what do you speak? We have taken nothing from you or anyone from Muspellsheim," answered Narfi.

"Liar! Sons of Odin Allfather, your warriors, led by Thor, entered my realm uninvited and stole The Warlock's Eye from me! For that, you will be my prisoners! Perhaps Odin will bargain for your lives and return what is mine!" With a wide swipe of his hand, Surt signaled for his guards to take the trio to his dungeon. The guards shoved them down rocky steps into a vast, smoky chamber lined with barred cells. They tossed them into the first available one and left.

"Even if Odin knew where we were, he would never bargain with Surt," moaned Vali. He sat on one of the two benches provided as furnishings for the cell. The other two sat as well, backs against the hot rocks of the prison. Narfi and Vali slipped out of their evening jackets, and unbuttoned their shirts in an effort to cool off.

"Oh, it's too hot to think," groaned Narfi. "Maybe he will send a message to Odin, and maybe word will get back to Father. Odin may do nothing, but Father would come, surely."

Jorda looked doubtful. "We don't know when this theft occurred. What if it happened before you were born? Time has no meaning when we cross the threshold of the door," she reminded him. "Such a demand for ransom, for three unheard of, so-called citizens of Asgard would go completely ignored. I'm afraid we must find our own way out again." She looked down at her hands, and a tear ran down her cheek.

Vali pulled her to his chest, hugging her. "It will be alright," he whispered. "After all, we're Loki's sons."

Narfi looked at his brother and sighed deeply. His brother was always so hopeful, so positive. He, on the other hand, was a "glass half empty" sort of fellow. "So," he said with a smile, "what's the first thing you're going to do when we get back to Asgard?"

Vali stared, for a moment puzzled, then he gave a quiet chuckle. "I believe I would eat an entire ox and sleep under the stars, breathing in the sweet air of Asgard!"

"I would draw a bath and soak for hours, and then I would saddle up Skaldra and ride for miles," said Jorda.

The three continued to talk this way for a while, then settled into silence. A jail-keeper arrived with some disgusting looking food in some bowls on a tray. They each took a bowl and dug their fingers into the gruel, having been deprived of any utensils. The food was tasteless, but helped to fill their empty stomachs. At least, they concluded, Surt hadn't planned to starve them to death while down in his dungeon. The small bit of food was enough to make them drowsy and they were soon asleep.

Narfi woke first, and he gazed at the figures of his brother and Jorda as they slept on the bench. Vali lay on his back with Jorda lying on top of him, her head resting on his chest. Narfi felt a small pang of regret, as he began to sense the beginnings of a small wedge being placed between him and his twin brother. He cursed himself for such thoughts and vowed to be happy that Vali and Jorda had found one another. Of course there would be women in their lives. He simply hadn't been prepared to face the fact just yet. The sound of the jail-keeper approaching woke the other two who sat up abruptly.

The jail-keeper placed a key into the lock and opened the heavy door. "The King needs your…" He paused and grinned. "…Services. He has guests he wants to entertain and guess what? You're the entertainment." He laughed as he pulled the three adolescents from the cell. He pushed them roughly down the corridor towards the exit of the dungeon. They were shoved up several flights of stairs, which finally ended in a sort of antechamber. Several guards grabbed Jorda, wrenching her from Vali, who demanded her release. They laughed cruelly at him as they held him back. Then they commanded that he and Narfi pick up shields and swords, but they watched the boys closely to make certain they didn't turn and attack. Now armed but outnumbered, the boys were shoved into an arena. In the center stood Jorda, lashed to a post.

Before Narfi could stop him, Vali ran into the arena towards Jorda. At that moment, an enormous lion with a mane of fire leapt towards him. Narfi ran at the beast, slicing off his fiery tail with one swipe of his sword. The lion roared and turned on him. "Vali!" Narfi cried. "A little help, brother!"

Vali whirled about and rushed to save his brother. He swung his sword at the lion's haunches just as it lunged towards Narfi and slashed into its thigh. The lion roared in pain, standing ready to charge between the two of them. It then spied the helpless Jorda, tied to the pole. Snarling, it leapt over Vali's head towards the girl. As it leapt, Vali raised his sword, ripping the creature down its middle. Flaming lava poured from the wound as the beast fell down dead. Vali jumped aside just in time to avoid his own fiery death. The brothers ran to each other, standing back to back, their swords at the ready. Seeing no other threat, Vali ran to Jorda and cut her bindings. Vali and Narfi kept her between them, crouched for the next attack. Surt looked down on them indifferently from his seat above the crowd. He sighed and motioned for his guards to return them to their cell.

They found themselves locked away once more, and Jorda trembled uncontrollably. Vali did his best to console her. Narfi sat down hard on the bench, putting his head in his hands. "By the gods, Vali, we have to get out of here. There must be a way," he said through his hands.

"But how?" asked Vali. "We have no magic here. Neither does Jorda. She said she couldn't communicate with the beast. We have been gone for days now. They must be searching for us back in Asgard. Someone must discover what happened to us. Our only hope is that Father finds the room and rescues us."

Narfi believed that each time they returned to the room, it was at the moment they had just left. In Asgard time then, they had been gone only minutes. There hadn't been time for anyone to miss them. He thought more about Surt and his ransom demand. All he wanted was The Warlock's Eye. What if he could promise to deliver it? He stared at his brother, so like staring into a mirror. In a flash, he had a plan. "I've got it!" he shouted, face beaming. "I know how to get out of here!"

Vali looked back at him in surprise. "What? How?" he asked. Jorda also stared quizzically at Narfi.

"Just play along. I'm pretty sure this plan will work," Narfi said.

"Pretty sure? How much is pretty sure?" Vali looked doubtful.

"I'd say ninety to ninety five percent sure," Narfi replied.

Vali looked unconvinced, then shrugged. "Well, we've face worse odds, I suppose," he said. "Are you going to share this plan with us?"

Narfi thought a moment. "No," he said. "I think it will be more convincing if you're left in the dark. Just trust me," he added. Banging on the prison cell's bars, Narfi yelled for the jail keeper. "Hey, jail-keep!" he shouted. "I know a way to get your King's precious artifact back to him! Bring me to him now!"

Though apprehensive, Jorda and Vali remained silent as the jail-keeper arrived to see what all the ruckus was about.

"What are you yelling about, Asgardian scum?" the jail-keeper sneered.

"I said, I know of a way to get The Warlock's Eye back from Asgard for your King," Narfi repeated.

The jail keeper eyed him with suspicion. "I'll give him your message, but if this is a trick, I'll skin you alive myself." With that, he turned and left.

The three sat and waited. Narfi paced the floor, face grave, hand over his mouth as he remained deep in thought, going over every possible scenario of his plan. Hours later, the jail-keeper and a dozen guards returned to their cell. Narfi grabbed the bars as the keeper unlocked the door.

The jail-keeper ordered two of the guards to flank Narfi's sides while the others were to surround the rest. The group marched up to Surt's throne room, where Narfi was pushed to his knees in front of the King. "The jail-keeper says you have a message for me, something about returning the Eye. I will hear you, but if this is some effort to trick me, the consequences will not be pleasant." Surt stared hard at the small figure of Narfi, bent in supplication on his knees.

"Yes, My Lord, but there is a problem. We arrived here by some strange accident. We're quite sure our absence is unnoticed on Asgard. Any request for ransom on your part will surely fall on deaf ears. But if you can send us to Asgard, we know where The Eye is kept and we can retrieve it and bring it to you in return for our freedom." Narfi studied Surt's face, and saw interest there.

Surt smiled cruelly at Narfi. "I will send two of you back, little Asgardian. One of you will stay here, as insurance," he said.

"Of course, My Lord. The girl should stay here, while my brother and I return," Narfi said.

Vali looked in shock at his brother, but said nothing. With all his might he was putting his trust in Narfi.

"Or perhaps my brother Vali should stay. As a grandson of Odin, he may be a more valuable hostage." Narfi's mind was racing, praying to the gods that Surt would take the bait.

"Perhaps, better yet, you should stay here, little one. You seem all the too anxious to leave the others behind. I shall send your brother and the girl to fetch The Eye. If they do not return promptly, I shall personally dip you into the molten River of Muspellsheim inches at a time, just to watch you melt."

Narfi looked anxious. "But, really, I should be one of the ones to go," he said. Surt grinned at Narfi's discomfort.

"I have made my decision. You shall stay."

Narfi paused. "Yes, I suppose it would be the same, if Vali went instead of me," he replied, wringing his hands. "But, my lord, you will promise that they will be delivered safely, and that not one bit of them, not so much as a hair or flake of skin shall remain here while they retrieve your Eye?" he begged.

Surt chuckled at the request. "Not so much as a fingernail, little Asgardian, shall be left behind." Surt motioned for his guards to take Vali and Jorda to the portal to Asgard.

Vali shouted, "No! Narfi, you mustn't sacrifice yourself!"

"If you return quickly with The Warlock's Eye, then no one will be sacrificed," Narfi answered coldly. "Just don't screw this up. My life depends on it," he added.

Surt smiled at Vali's anguished face. "Go now, and do your brother's bidding, little Asgardian. Return with that which is mine, and I will return all of you safely back to Asgard."

Vali knew this was a lie. He was sure that even if he could return with The Eye, they would be executed. Narfi looked hard at his brother, nodding almost imperceptibly. Against all his instincts, Vali turned and followed the guards to the portal room. He and Jorda stepped up to a platform, and a gatekeeper, the Muspellsheim equivalent to Heimdall, drove his sword into the port key. Seconds later, Vali, Jorda, and Narfi stood back in the room of doors. Vali stared in disbelief at his brother, and then grabbed him in a crushing hug. "How did you do it?" he screamed. "How in the name of the gods did you manage it?"

Narfi was grinning from ear to ear. "I wasn't entirely sure it would work," he said, "but you and I are identical. We share the same hair, the same skin, and even the same fingerprints. Our blood is identical. Surt couldn't send one of us off entirely-- we are inseparable. At least, that was what I had hoped. That's why I had to trick him into 'forcing' me to stay. I didn't want you left there if the plan didn't work."

Jorda threw her arms around Narfi. "I knew you weren't so selfish," she whispered into his ear. "I knew you wouldn't really sacrifice your brother...or me." She dropped her arms from his neck, stepping back to Vali's side. Narfi felt himself blush and found a reason to turn away.

"We're getting closer," Narfi said. "Only three doors left to Asgard." He stroked one of the remaining unmarked doors, hoping to feel some sign that it was the door to Asgard.

"That was brilliant, brother. You think just like Father," Vali remarked.

"It was pretty brilliant the way you took out that beast, brother. My first reaction would have been to duck!" Narfi clapped his brother's shoulder. "We all make a fantastic team. We really are going to make it out of here, aren't we?"

Jorda spoke. "You had doubt? How could you doubt the sons of Loki?"

"Mainly because we *are* the sons of Loki. You know, Chaos and all that. I'm always surprised when things do turn out alright," Narfi said, smirking.

"Narfi, when did you become such a skeptic? Things always turn out. In the end." Vali laughed, realizing that his brother did indeed have a point.

Jorda sat down and leaned against one of the doors. "Could we rest a bit? I want to get home again, too, but could we take a break, for just a while?" Her eyes were weary and she felt weak.

Vali lay down next to her, his head on her lap. Looking up at her, Vali asked, "Do you still want to return to Alfheim? Would it be so terrible for you to stay in Asgard, now?"

Jorda looked away, carefully pondering Vali's question. She had grown fond of Vali and of Narfi. But she missed her mother and her home. She had done what her mother had hoped she would do. She had learned not to spread her negative emotions to those around her. She looked down at Vali and smiled weakly. "Asgard is not so unpleasant now," Jorda said, stroking his hair, "but Asgard is not my home."

It was not the answer Vali had hoped for. He tried to hide his disappointment and smiled back at her. "But perhaps you'll come to visit more often now. Perhaps I could come to visit you," he thought out loud. Vali wasn't sure, but he thought he was falling in love.

"Of course I'll visit," she promised. "We'll keep in touch. How could I not stay friends with the man who saved me from the jaws of a fire-lit lion?" she teased. She had said it; she had referred to their relationship as "friends." She was not ready for anything beyond that. The fact that she had any friends at all was new to her. When she walked into a room of her peers on Alfheim, they had either shied away from her because of her own shyness, or wound up angry and fighting one another because of her anger. She felt that she needed more time.

Narfi overheard the conversation and knew his brother's heart was breaking. He was proud of Jorda, however. Her honesty at this point would save Vali much worse heartache later. He turned and lay on his side, head propped on one elbow, sketching into the dusty floor with his free hand. The room was dim and without a thought, he conjured his cat light. It appeared immediately, sitting quietly by his side. He stared at it in surprise. Vali and Jorda squinted in the sudden light. "I forgot that we could use magic here," Narfi said.

Vali tried to conjure a chair, but nothing happened. Next, he tried for a sword, but still no results. Then he held out his hand, and the blue flame rose above his palm. "I suppose we may conjure only nonmaterial things," he observed. "Perhaps, if we concentrate together, we can get a message to Father," suggested Vali.

Narfi felt the idea was ludicrous, but he didn't want to disappoint his brother. "It's at least worth a try," he agreed. "We'll ask him to come to the cave. Jorda, let's all join hands and concentrate. All of us, picture Dad standing outside the portal into the room." They joined hands and closed their eyes, concentrating hard on the image Narfi suggested.

CHAPTER 6

Loki stood at the rim of the vast upper terrace that overlooked most of Asgard. Though still resented and untrusted by most of her citizenry, Loki had learned to ignore his detractors and was enjoying the life he had with his bride and his sons. He looked toward the forest, where he knew the boys had planned to go that day. Though some way off, he thought he sighted a lone horse grazing in the fields just in front of the forest. He squinted and brought his hand up over his eyes to see better, but the horse, if that was what it was, was gone. He felt a slight unease, but did not pursue it. The children had only just left, so he felt sure they hadn't had time to fall into any danger, yet. If they didn't return soon, he would take Sigyn with him and ride out to look for them.

* * *

Back inside the room of doors, Narfi first broke the circle by releasing his grip on Vali's and Jorda's hands. "Either we reached him, or we didn't," he said. "We've wasted enough time. I'll pick the next door." He walked over to the one of the four remaining doors, preparing to open it. "Well?" he asked, waiting for the two to join him.

Vali hesitated. "Perhaps we should wait a while, to see if Father heard us or anything."

Narfi scoffed. "You don't think we actually accomplished anything, do you?" He stood defiant, head back, staring down at his brother.

"Narfi, why all the anger? We've overcome the most unbelievable hardships and returned unscathed. We have reason to be proud. We have no reason to give up. We'll make it back. What has changed you all of a sudden?" Vali asked.

Narfi did not answer, turning his gaze to the floor. "I don't know, Vali. I wish I was as sure as you, but this may not be any sort of test at all. What if it's a trap? What if one of these doors is meant to hold a task that is totally insurmountable and we've just been lucky not to stumble upon it yet? If Father was going to feel anything from us, he would have already felt it a long time ago. This place; it's cursed. We're never meant to leave, I just know."

Vali was quiet. "Well, then, why don't we just lie down and die right here? Why bother to go through another door? What's the point, Narfi?"

Narfi looked away from his brother's troubled eyes. "Because... Because it is better to die quickly than to die a slow death of starvation and failure. I would rather die a hero's death than to just lie down and sleep for eternity," he answered.

"Alright," said Vali. "Perhaps the next time we leave some realm it will be to enter Valhalla. Whatever we do, brother, we will do it together." Vali and Jorda stood next to Narfi. "So, open the door, brother."

*   *   *

Narfi opened the door to a dark and barren landscape. "Jotunheim," the three said in unison. They crouched down, spying King Thrym sitting on his throne in the distance. They spotted a winding path that led down away from their precarious slab of teetering rock and began their decent with care. They came to an expanse of bleak, frost-covered land but thought they saw what looked like greenish, stunted trees in the distance. They crept towards the trees. They stopped once in a while, crouching low to the ground to make sure they had not been seen. The ground became less rocky. Bits of moss and lichen cushioned their steps.

"These plants are very ancient," Jorda whispered. "They are the most primitive of all growing things. It's as though this land is trying to recover itself, to regenerate."

They came to the edge of the strange little trees and stepped among them, feeling easier with the additional cover. As they walked deeper, the trees got larger and more familiar looking. The dark clouds overhead seemed a bit thinner, allowing more light to filter through. They came to a clearing and at its far end sat a neat hut. They ducked down as a woman walked out carrying a bucket in one hand. The woman was quite lovely. Her hair was long and black, her figure trim, and her face very pleasant to look at.

"She looks okay," said Vali.

"Looks can be deceiving, brother, as you well know," Narfi said. "There are no humans or Aesirians living in Jotunheim that I ever heard of. She must be a giantess who has disguised herself for some reason."

"Perhaps to lure people like us?" suggested Jorda. "Your brother's right, Vali. We should be careful." She kept herself down and peered from behind a tree.

"I hope you know that I can hear every word," said the woman. "Come out of the shadows. I won't hurt you, Asgardians."

Vali was first to straighten and walk into the open. The woman looked at him and dropped her bucket. She appeared flabbergasted for a moment, then came to some sort of realization and beckoned to him. "You looked for a moment like someone I once knew," she said. "I see now that you are not he. Perhaps you are his son? Is your father the Asgardian god known as Loki, the god of Mischief?"

"You know of Loki?" Vali asked, wary of her knowledge.

"Of course," she answered. "Loki and I were…" She hesitated, and then said, "We were great friends, once."

"And now? Are you great friends now?" Vali wanted to test the waters before admitting who he really was. Narfi came up behind Vali, Jorda following him.

"Twins," she proclaimed, spotting Narfi as he drew up next to Vali. "Multiple births. How odd," she mused. "Walk with me. I'm just going to fetch some water. One of you boys can carry it back for me. My name is Angrboda, and this is where I live. It used to be as bleak here as the rest of Jotunheim," she explained, "but since I met your father, I've had a different view of life. I prefer color now, and living things, and light." She showed them a stone well filled with crystal clear water. "Perhaps you would have some tea with me?"

Vali noticed sadness in the woman's eyes. He felt drawn to her and a great desire to help her in any way he could. He took the bucket from her gently and plunged it into the water till it was full. Then taking her arm, they walked back to her cottage. Narfi and Jorda followed a few steps behind. The two glanced at one another. Neither knew quite what to make of this strange new friendship between Vali and Angrboda.

They found the interior of the home to be warm and inviting. The chairs were covered with soft cushions in pastel colors. On the small table in the dining area sat a wooden bowl full of golden apples. Vali helped Angrboda fill her kettle with the spring water and hung it over the fire burning in the hearth. Angrboda withdrew four dainty cups and saucers from the cupboard. They joined Vali and Jorda, already sitting at the table.

"This is very kind of you, Angrboda," said Jorda. "We're not used to being welcomed like this."

"I can't imagine why not," replied Angrboda. "You all seem like such perfectly nice young people. Why have you come to Jotunheim? You must know that there is no love lost between most of the Jotun and any of the Aesirs. Neither Odin nor Thor has much use for us, either. There was a time when your father was our friend, but he has distanced himself as well."

Narfi sensed there was something Angrboda was keeping from them. "How well did you know our father?" he asked.

The woman shifted in her seat as she pondered how to answer Narfi's question. "It was all a long, long time ago. Your father was distraught. He believed his family was dead. He blamed his father and yet, loved him dearly at the same time. He needed someone to…to comfort him. I filled that need for a while. But in the end, his loyalties remained with

Asgard, in spite of all the cruelties they heaped upon him." Her eyes turned hard. "Even after they…"

"They what?" urged Narfi. "Tell us, please." He and Vali had overheard more than a few conversations about their father and his exploits after they and their mother had been banished.

Vali placed a hand over the woman's, reassuring her that whatever she had to say would be all right. They knew that Odin had tried to drive their father mad and had nearly succeeded. "I think it would help you, too, to talk about it," he said.

Angrboda looked into Vali's eyes, those eyes so like his father's, and began her story. "As I said, your father was nearly insane with grief. He had performed many tasks for his father in an effort to please him, thinking that somehow, this would ease his pain. He still held on to a tiny shred of hope that it was all a terrible mistake and that you were still alive, hidden from him until he could win his father's approval again. The Asgardians always blamed Loki for everything that went wrong in Asgard, even those things that were not his responsibility." She smiled, and continued.

"Finally, he could take no more, and came here, to Jotunheim, the land of his birth."

Narfi and Vali swallowed hard, remembering their blue skin at the touch of the Frost Giant's casket. "So he really is part Jotun?" asked Narfi.

"Yes. Odin stole him when he was a newborn babe, believing that he had been abandoned. Of course, Odin's prophesy told him a Jotun child would drive the final destruction of Ragnarok, so having his own little Jotun in the House of Odin fit nicely into his plan. He used your father, manipulated him, and drove him to madness. That is what pushed him here, into my arms." She stood, poured hot water into the tea cups, and then sat down to continue.

She was quiet a moment as they sipped their tea. Angrboda was worried that this might be too much knowledge. There were some things that a child simply should not know about his parents. She began, "Maybe you should leave it alone. You really don't need to hear all this, do you?"

"I do," said Narfi. His face was hard to read. He wore an expression somewhere between resolution and resignation. In other words, his face showed the turmoil roiling in his head. In a moment he was going to have to face the fact that his father had weaknesses. It is difficult and sometimes traumatic for children to learn that their parents have feet of clay. It wasn't as though his father had ever lied to him. Loki was the first to admit he had imperfections. It was one thing to know a beloved parent was not perfect. It was another thing altogether to see that imperfection up close, complete with all the gory details.

With a sigh, Angrboda began her tale. "As I told you, your father was suffering almost unbearable grief after he was falsely informed that you and your mother were dead. He would drink and pick fights just so he could be beaten, hoping his physical pain would mask the pain in his heart. After weeks of this self-flagellation, he started to believe the three of you might still be alive somewhere and that Odin was hiding you to punish him for not being a good enough son. Odin took advantage of him and told him to work out a plan that would lead to the destruction of one of his rivals, the giant Thiassi. In Loki's plan, he would give him Iduna, the keeper of the golden apples that maintained the Aesir's youth and good health. He would then rescue her, incite Thiassi to give him chase, and lure him to his death. The giants would not retaliate, because it would look as though Thiassi had stolen Iduna himself and his death would be justifiable. All happened just as Loki had planned. Iduna was forever safe, having been planted as a great tree within the walls of Asgard, and Thiassi was dead, but all those vain, silly Asgardians remembered was that Loki had abducted Iduna and caused them to age for a few weeks." Angrboda's face was dark with anger and hatred for the Aesir.

"But Odin told them it was all his idea, didn't he? He couldn't allow his son to take the blame for a plot that he himself had instigated, could he?" Jorda asked She couldn't believe that any father could allow his own son to be so mistreated.

Angrboda gave a mirthless laugh. "Ha! Odin would have Loki roasted and served to the gods for dinner if it suited his purposes. Odin had his own plan in mind. Ragnarok must occur at the hands of Loki and to make him do it, Odin had to drive him insane with hatred of Asgard and all the nine Realms. Without knowing it, Odin even had me to play a part in Yggdrasil's final destruction." Her eyes welled with tears. "After the reception Loki received upon the return of Iduna, he abandoned Asgard. He returned to Jotunheim and found me as he roved the countryside, mad with rage. I saw him as he wandered, and thought he was interesting looking." She smiled, her eyes far away in memory. "I made myself into what I hoped would be interesting to him and invited him into this cottage, which I now call my home. I encouraged him to talk and he unburdened himself to me. I held him, comforted him, and we…" Her eyes fell on the children. "We made love."

The color rose in Vali's cheeks as he worked the cuticles of his fingers. Narfi's elbows rested on the table and he held his head in his hands, which shielded his face.

"You fell in love with him, didn't you?" asked Jorda. "How romantic! But, how tragic!"

"How tragic indeed," Angrboda agreed. "I did love him but his thoughts, his heart, were always for Sigyn. His feelings for me were more of shame than affection. He stayed with me until our children were born…"

Vali and Narfi both jumped with this news. "Children? There are others besides us? Where?" demanded Narfi.

Angrboda's tears stained her face. "My children, our children were…" She searched for the right word. "They were special. Your father looks as he does because he has been Aesir since a newborn infant. I look like an Aesir because of a spell I maintain on myself. The effect of maintaining such a spell on oneself during pregnancy can create certain changes in one's offspring," she explained. "Loki stayed with me out of a sense of duty. He may have made room for me somewhere in his heart. I don't know. He was attentive to me and took care of me. When the children were born, he didn't seem disappointed, in spite of their appearance."

"How many other children does he have?" Jorda asked. She decided to ask the pertinent questions, since the boys seemed to have lost their ability to speak.

"I had the one birth, but gave him three children. First was Hela, beautiful of face, but with a body half putrid and rotten with death. The second to come was also the most strange--Jormundgand, the serpent. Lastly came the wolf pup Fenrir, who grew to enormous size. Odin knew of my children, believing they would help Loki at the time of Ragnarok, but he feared them and ordered Tyr and his brutish friends to take care of them. As I slept, they stole into the nursery. When Tyr first laid eyes on the decayed lower body of Hela, he was so repulsed that he slit her throat and left her for dead. The others took Jormundgand and flung him to the seas of Midgard. Tyr took a liking to the gentle wolf pup Fenrir, and took him back to Asgard with them. A sword was taken to me as well, but as you see, I survived." Angrboda washed her hands across her face, trying to compose herself so that she could continue.

Jorda placed a hand over Angrboda's. "If this is too painful, you needn't go on," she said. Her heart ached for this woman, another cruel victim of old Odin's madness.

Angrboda took a deep breath and smiled. "No, I want to finish," she said. "The boys deserve to hear this. Loki visited me and nursed me to health. In spite of all that had happened, in spite of the banishment of Hela to Helheim, and of Jormundgand to Midgard, and the attempt on my life, he continued to avow his love of and loyalty to Asgard. He told me there had to be a purpose and that he was sure Odin would finally confide in him if only he could prove himself worthy. It was then that I threw him out. I was sick of his pity. I ordered him to leave and to never return. The cruelest injury of all was the look of relief on Loki's face. He took the blame for all that had occurred and begged my forgiveness. I believe he was sincere…" Her voice was small, her eyes staring into nothingness. With a slight jerk, she brought herself back into focus.

"Loki was often gone from Asgard after that," she said. "He travelled often to Earth, where the people were simpler and made no demands of him. I heard he once saved a child there, but I digress. Fenrir had grown to an enormous size but remained gentle and had as much intelligence as you or I. Tyr liked to parade him around Asgard as if he had control over this massive beast. He placed heavy chains around his neck to magnify the effect of Fenrir's ferocity. One day, Tyr was showing off his control over the beast by sticking his arm into Fenrir's mouth and 'commanding' him not to bite down. At the same time, Tyr jangled the heavy chains and one broken link, sharply pointed, sank into Fenrir's neck. Fenrir snapped his jaws shut in pain and took Tyr's hand off, as well. From that point onward, Tyr considered Fenrir dangerous and had him chained deep beneath the earth. Loki begged for his release, but Odin refused."

"Hela has become the Queen of the underworld and seems quite at peace with her lot. Jormundgand swims in an eternal circle around the Earth and seems quite happy. Finally, during that brief period while your father was King,

Fenrir was released to Jotunheim. He sits at Court with King Thrym now, and though he has lost his innocence, he seems content."

The group sat in silence, digesting the mournful story related by Angrboda. Narfi pushed his chair back and rose to walk outside. Vali shot a worried glance at Jorda and followed.

"What goes, brother," Vali asked softly.

Narfi stood still for a few moments longer. He turned and held up his fist for his brother to bump with his own. "That's a lot to take in," he remarked.

Vali laid his hand on Narfi's shoulder. "Will you be okay?" he asked.

"Okay?" asked Narfi incredulously. "Okay? Vali, our sister is the goddess of the Underworld. Our brother is the wolf-man parents warn their children about at night, and yet another brother is… is, 'the Loch Ness Monster'! That, I believe, is the definition of a dysfunctional family!" Narfi's face was flush with rage as his voice rose. "Oh, and while we were freezing our asses off in Siberia, Father was shacking up with a Jotun giantess! Oh, yes, brother, I'm okay! I am effing fantastic!"

"Father thought we were dead, Narfi. You can't blame him. None of this was his fault…"

Narfi turned on his brother. "Of course it's all his fault, Vali! He could have fought for us! He could have swept us all away before Odin sent us to Siberia! He had the power to reduce Fingardin to ash the day Mother was taken away to Scandia! But he didn't. He just sat there and let it all happen. And then he fucked that monster and allowed her to bring not one, but three monsters into the world!" Tears were now streaming down Narfi's face.

Vali stood motionless. "Well, to be honest, they're only our *half*-sister and brothers," he said.

Narfi stared at his brother as if he were completely insane. Vali smiled at him and extended his hand. Narfi looked down at his brother's hand as if he couldn't recognize it. Finally, his shoulders relaxed, and with eyes closed, he grabbed Vali's hand and pulled him to his chest. They gave each other a quick embrace before separating with a slap to each other's back. "You don't have a problem with all this?" Narfi asked.

"Maybe a little, way back when. But Mother knew Dad did what he could. He was a Prince of Asgard, Narfi. If he had reacted too rashly, there could have been war. Odin was the one pulling all the strings. If you're going to blame someone for all our misery, blame him."

Narfi rubbed his eyes, absorbing his brother's words. He thought about his own recent outburst, wondering where it had come from. Obviously, he had been harboring this deep seated resentment for years. Apparently his love for his father had been balanced precariously on a thin line bordering hate. He wanted to be as powerful as his father, to be as strong, as great a sorcerer, as brilliant. To discover that Loki was so flawed meant that he too was flawed, didn't it? Such a revelation made his love quickly turn to hate. If his father couldn't be faultless, he had to be reviled. Narfi felt himself sinking into these dark thoughts as one would sink into mud. He allowed himself to be swallowed up in self-pity and loathing. He followed Vali slowly back into the house.

Angrboda was busy setting out plates for her guests. She had slices of cold meat, sautéed orange and yellow vegetables, thickly sliced bread, and fresh butter. Jorda and Vali were putting out knives and forks and helping set the table for dinner. Angrboda glanced up as Narfi entered, then hurriedly looked away. Narfi's cheeks reddened as he remembered his rant outside. He realized she must have overheard. He walked up behind her and whispered, "I'm sorry, Angrboda, I didn't mean…"

She turned and stopped him. "Yes, you did, but I understand why. You're hurting and you want someone to blame. Right now, it's me and your father. After a while, you'll want to blame yourself. But answer me this, little Asgardian, what does it matter? Will you receive peace by assigning blame? Will it make your pain go away? Yes, you were mistreated. So was your father, and so was I. We all were. Don't waste your life trying to find some sort of justice in all of this; there is none. Do yourself a favor, and forgive. This is the only way you will truly find peace." With that, she brought a large bowl of buttery fried apples over to the table and invited all to sit and eat.

Sheepishly, Narfi joined the others at the table. He filled his plate with the delicious food Angrboda had prepared for them just realizing how empty his stomach had been. The more he ate, the more he felt inclined to take Angrboda's advice. Between asking for this or that dish to be passed, the three complemented and thanked her for her wonderful meal. They laughed and playfully picked food off of each other's plates. Now completely sated, they leaned back, relishing the fullness in their bellies.

"Alright," announced Jorda. "I'll wash, Vali will dry, and Narfi, you put things away. We'll all clear the table." She stood, picking up two of the empty plates.

Vali and Narfi looked at each other. "Are you mad? Are you asking the sons of Loki, Prince of Asgard, to do woman's work?" demanded Vali, with a wide grin.

"Vali, let us repair to the drawing room, and leave these ladies to their housework," replied Narfi.

Vali looked up in time to be hit in the face with a dish towel. "I wash, you dry," Jorda said. "You, Narfi, put things away. Now both of you, help me bring these to the basin." Laughing, the boys did as they were told. Angrboda supervised, sitting at the table with a cup of tea. Within no time, the kitchen was cleared and cleaned.

The day had turned to night. Angrboda brought them pillows and blankets to camp out on the floor. As she was about to retire to her own bedroom, Vali asked, "Angrboda, we need to find a way back. Is there a way that we can get to Asgard from here?"

"Why don't you call to Heimdall? You should be able to return by the Bifrost. Tell me again how you got here," she replied.

"It's rather a long story. We found a portal and when we went through, we entered this room full of doors. Each door led to one of the Realms, but each time we escaped, instead of returning to Asgard, we wound up back in the room again. We never know where, or when for that matter, we'll go when we pass through one of the doors. Jotunheim seems to be closest to the present of all the Realms we've visited so far."

"That's very strange magic, isn't it?" Angrboda commented. "Perhaps you're cloaked when you travel. If that's the case, it would be as if you didn't exist. There are other ways, of course…" She looked off into the distance, thinking. "If you were with another Aesir, you could sort of hitch a ride with him."

"Great idea, but there are no Aesirs in Jotunheim, are there?" Narfi asked.

"Well, there's one. At least, he's part Aesir," remarked Angrboda.

The trio was startled at this revelation, until Narfi recalled Angrboda's tale. "You're talking about Fenrir, aren't you?"

"Yes. He lived on Asgard most of his life. He was considered a citizen of Asgard up until the incident with Tyr. I believe he can still travel freely between the Realms, if he should so desire," Angrboda explained. "Get some rest. You'll work it out tomorrow." With that, she walked into her room and shut the door.

The next morning, Jorda, Vali, and Narfi woke to the sounds and scents of Angrboda cooking their breakfast. They folded their blankets and gathered their pillows and put them back into the trunk from which Angrboda had withdrawn them. After breakfast, they sat around the table and discussed their options.

"Do you think you could summon Fenrir?" Vali asked Jorda.

"I could try, but he's not totally animal, is he? He's more of a person in his mind. He has intelligence beyond that of normal animals. But I'll give it a go." She closed her eyes, concentrating on sending a message to Fenrir. She felt her thoughts reaching out, searching for their target. She noticed a slight pull, like someone was searching back. A moment later, they had connected.

"Child of Jord, why do you disturb my rest?" asked a low, growling voice, heard only to Jorda.

"Forgive me, My Lord," she apologized. "I am the daughter of Jord. My name is Jorda, and I am a cousin of Loki." She waited for a response.

Finally he answered. "I am aware of the relationship between Jord and my father," he growled. "We are very distantly related, at best. What do you want, Alfheimir?" He sounded impatient.

"Fenrir Lokison, I am trapped here in Jotunheim with your half-brothers, Vali and Narfi. We beg your help." Even though they were probably miles apart, Jorda was physically trembling at the sound of Fenrir's thoughts. She sensed that this once gentle being had become more feral since his incarceration underground.

*　　*　　*

Fenrir stood from his resting place and began pacing his room. He avoided contact with all things Aesir, and this intrusion troubled him. His father visited him often while he was chained deep in the caves. Loki always brought plenty of meat and often brought books and news of the outside world. Loki's first act as King was to free his son and he invited Fenrir to live with him in Asgard, but he refused. He held too much hatred for the Asgardians to trust that he would not strike out at them in an uncontrolled fit of rage. He chose his mother's world, instead. He was more comfortable with the cold and darkness, and he was accepted here without reservation. He had almost forgotten his old life until this little Alfheim brat decided to reach out to him. "Are you with my mother?" he asked.

Jorda gulped. "Y-yes," she answered. "Please, we need the help of another Aesir in order to get back…"

"I am no Aesir!" Though these were only silent thoughts being sent to her mind, Jorda jumped at the violence behind the words. Fenrir continued, "If only an Aesir can help you, then you are out of luck, little Jorda. Now, leave me be. I want nothing to do with any Aesir, ever again."

"Please, Fenrir, we only want to go home. Please do this, and I swear, we will never bother you again," pleaded Jorda.

Fenrir didn't believe there was anything he could do for these children. He lowered his head, heaving a great sigh. He knew what it was like to long for home and to feel helpless and trapped. Reluctantly, he decided to do what he could. If nothing else, he would finally meet his two half-brothers. "Alright, I will come, but don't expect miracles. I doubt there will be anything I can do for you."

It wasn't long before Jorda began to feel the hairs on the back of her neck stand up. "He's here," she said. A moment later, there was a knock at the door.

Angrboda opened the door to her son. Fenrir stood on his hind legs and they embraced, and a beaming Angrboda turned and introduced him to the group. "Fenrir, this is Jorda.

And these are your brothers, Vali and Narfi." They all stood and Vali strode to the enormous wolf, extending his hand.

"I'm Vali," he said. "This is Narfi. People seem to have a hard time telling us apart," he added. "It's wonderful to meet you."

Fenrir looked at the proffered hand, finally taking it in his own. Fenrir's hand resembled a wolf's paw, but with long pointed fingers like a man's. They shook, but the wolf remained cautious. Narfi offered his hand as well, and Fenrir shook it, too. "How do you think I can help you, Asgardians?" he snarled.

Angrboda answered for the three of them. "Only you can beckon Heimdall to open the Bifrost. The magic that brought them here has cloaked them. Heimdall cannot hear or see them, but you are the son of a Prince of Asgard. He cannot refuse you. Call Heimdall, and take the children with you. You needn't stay. Once they have been delivered, you can return instantly. It isn't so much to ask, my son."

The wolf-man gave his mother's request a great deal of thought. He promised himself he would never set foot in Asgard again, not even to step onto the Rainbow Bridge leading into the city. He doubted that Heimdall would respond to his voice, son of a prince or not. The young trio was gazing anxiously at him. How could he refuse? "I will try, for you, Mother. Come along outside. We'll join hands, and I will summon Heimdall."

"Thank you, Fenrir," said Vali. "We all understand how much we're asking of you. We have no love for Heimdall, either. There is something you should know, however. We may not appear on the Bridge at your side. The magic usually puts us back in the chamber of doors like the one that led us to Jotunheim. We've been through all the Realms except Vanaheim and Svartalfaheim, not counting the last door, Asgard."

"If I arrive alone, I could find Father, and send him to help you," offered Fenrir.

"No!" shouted Narfi. Everyone turned to stare at him. "There's the whole space-time continuum thing," he insisted. "If we're here at a time that is, say, two months behind Asgard time, then we wouldn't have left yet. Father might think you were crazy. You might even run into the 'us' that was two months ago. I don't know what the consequences for something like that might be. It's better that you do like

Angrboda said. If we aren't beside you, just turn around and come back immediately."

The group remained silent, mouths agape. "You're sure about this, brother?" asked Vali.

"Of course I'm not sure about it, but I don't think we should take any risks. We only have two more doors. I think we should play this thing out," Narfi advised.

Vali looked at Fenrir. "Better do as he says; he's the brains," he said, smiling. Fenrir looked incredulous but promised to comply.

Once outside, the group joined hands. Fenrir called, "Heimdall, open the Bifrost." Nothing happened. "Heimdall, open the Bifrost!" he commanded. A few more seconds passed, when they were suddenly surrounded by a brilliant light, and then they were gone.

Opening their eyes, they all sighed at once. "Home again," moaned Jorda. "Hello, room," she twittered. "Hello, doors."

"Do you think he'll keep his promise?" asked Vali. "You've gotten me a little worried about this space-time continuum thing." He gave his brother a crooked smile.

"Laugh all you want, brother. I, for one, do not wish to mix science with magic. The consequences could be…" He searched for a word. "Epic." Narfi walked over to the last three doors, touching each one in turn.

"Okay, fine. Our choices today are Vanaheim and Svartalfaheim." Vali joined his brother, willing the doors to speak to them and announce which one led to Asgard.

"So, what will it be? Eeny, meeny, miney, moe?" asked Vali.

"That's what I just did," admitted Jorda. "It's this one." She laid a hand on the handle of one of the doors.

Vali held up a thumb, and his brother did the same. "Here goes nothing," announced Vali.

* * *

"Oh, crap," groaned Jorda as she surveyed their dark and rocky surroundings once they came through the door. "Svartalfaheim. Well, at least we know Vanaheim is next," she said.

They had walked into what was probably the main workshop of one of the kingdoms of the Dwarves. Dwarves were hammering metals and stoking fires. Some were pushing heavy carts piled with metal ore or coal. All were busy and hard at work. Vali leaned in close to the other two. "Let's just hope this isn't the kingdom of Brokk. If he knew Loki's sons were here, we would be dead meat for sure," he warned.

"Oh, is he the one…" began Jorda.

"Yeah, he's the one who sewed Dad's mouth shut. Not a nice guy," added Narfi.

They began to look for a place to hide. They crouched down and made their way along a ledge that seemed to lead to a cave or corridor. Once at the opening, they peered around the edge and determined it was safe to enter. The long hallway led down and the deeper they crept, the stronger the scent of cooking food. "Must be the kitchen," said Narfi. "Maybe we can overhear something useful there."

They were able to hide behind the cave entrance into the kitchen. There was so much noise and activity, they felt safe from detection. The Dwarves had to speak loudly to be heard over the din of clanging pots and chopping knives. To their relief, they overheard the name of King Ivaldi mentioned on several occasions. "Ivaldi was always rather fond of Father," Narfi said. "Perhaps we can reason with him to send us back."

Jorda turned to look at Narfi. "So, you think we should just go up to him and ask? That seems too simple. Every other realm has had us overcome some challenge or other. Perhaps we should be more cautious. Maybe we need to come up with a plan."

"Or maybe we're just finally getting lucky," whispered Vali. Narfi and Jorda both turned to face him. "Or not."

Narfi thought for a moment. "What if one of us goes, and the others should stay hidden and try to come up with a plan if the meeting doesn't work out," he suggested.

"No, we shouldn't split up. We do much better when we're together." Jorda said, biting her lip in concentration. "Dwarves are related to the Elves. I know that the Elven mines have secret passageways that lead to other Realms. Perhaps the Dwarves have them, too."

"Of course!" cried Narfi. "How else could they get their gifts and wares into the caves of Asgard? We'll have to keep an eye on the craftsmen as they finish their work. Maybe they'll lead us to one of these passageways."

"I have an idea," said Vali. "What if we went to Ivaldi and told him we wanted the Dwarves to make us something? Maybe we could ask for a gift for our parents. We could say it was for their anniversary. That way, we would have an excuse to be involved from start to finish."

"That's brilliant!" cried Narfi. "We might even convince him to let us deliver the gift in person! Vali, my brother, it seems that my vastly superior intelligence has finally started to rub off on you," he joked.

"My dear brother, your modesty is only exceeded by your enormous humility. I am blessed to grovel in your mighty shadow," answered Vali, with a laugh.

"Ah, I'm so glad that you finally see the light, brother, but I'll give you this--you are definitely the better looking." The three shared a few more laughs and began to creep back towards the Dwarves' work place. They looked for an entrance into the cave so as to look as though they had walked in from above ground. They found daylight, turned, and strode down into the cave again, this time right down the middle path with heads held high. Two armored Dwarves took up posts on either side, accompanying them into Ivaldi's chamber. King Ivaldi's throne sat high so that he might survey the entire workshop. He stared down at the young people with some curiosity.

"Loki's sons, as I live and breathe! Your father has bragged about you over many a flagon of ale, lads! Welcome to my kingdom, and tell me what brings you here?" The old Dwarf descended from his throne and approached his guests. As he neared the little party, he noticed Jorda for the first time. "And who is this fair maid? My boys, do you have a sister? Did that goat Loki produce such a beauty as this?" He took Jorda's hand to his lips and kissed her fingertips.

"You flatter me, My Lord," Jorda said. "I am but a distant cousin. My mother, the goddess Jord, has sent me to stay for a while with my cousins, and they were kind enough to bring me along with them to meet you."

Ivaldi's smile slipped into more of a leer as he stared up and down at Jorda. "How kind," he observed. "We must see that our guests are made most welcome," he continued, keeping her hand in his own.

"Your Highness," began Narfi, "we know that yours are the most skilled craftsmen in all of Yggdrasil. My brother Vali and I would ask that you make us a pair of chalices to give our parents in honor of their wedding anniversary."

Vali tried to casually take Jorda's free arm with his own. "Yes, Your Majesty. We would be most grateful."

"Your gratitude is most graciously appreciated, lads, but I'm afraid I will need more than that." He stopped, his face becoming shrewd. "I will give you your chalices, but you must promise to bring me something I deem of equal value."

Vali and Narfi looked at one another. They knew they could promise anything, because once back in the chamber of doors, they would be unreachable. Vali gave a little shrug, so Narfi answered, "Whatever you wish, My Lord. Once you have sent us back to Asgard with the gift, we will return with the object you desire." Narfi bent in a low bow to the King to show his utter sincerity.

"Done and done, then. My best craftsmen will begin immediately, but, for now, we must prepare the banquet hall for a celebration! We celebrate our new friends, Vali and Narfi Lokison, and their lovely cousin, Jorda." Ivaldi clapped his hands and dozens of Dwarves scurried about preparing for a great feast and celebration.

* * *

The Dwarves expended the same energy and enthusiasm for their play as they did for their work. There was music and dancing, laughter, and much, much drinking. They were especially taken with Jorda, since no women lived in any of the kingdoms of Svartalfaheim. She found them to be pleasant enough little men, so she obligingly danced with any who asked. The party lasted into the wee hours of the evening before the king announced that the celebration was officially at an end. He instructed his men to accompany the young guests to their rooms. Vali, Narfi, and Jorda all commented on the excellent food and drink, and thanked the King profusely. The King was pleased and bade them good night.

Vali and Narfi were settled into one room with Jorda placed into a room opposite theirs. They slept soundly and awoke early, anxious to see what progress Ivaldi's craftsmen had made. Vali knocked quietly on Jorda's door, but heard no response. Concerned, he knocked more loudly, but still she did not answer. He tried the latch and found the room to be unlocked. Once inside, he discovered that Jorda was missing. "Narfi, come quick!" he shouted.

Narfi responded immediately. They searched for any clue to Jorda's whereabouts but found nothing. Her bed hadn't been slept in and the room looked as though it had never been touched. "Maybe she arose early and went on to the workshop without us," suggested Narfi, though he didn't believe it for a second.

Vali glanced disdainfully at him. Narfi held up his hands in an 'I know, I know' kind of way. They hurried down the corridor and winding steps that led to Ivaldi's work room. The King was on his throne and beckoned them to approach.

"Ah, my boys, I trust you slept well after all the festivities last night?" he inquired.

"Yes, My Lord," answered Vali. "We were wondering, My Lord, if you had sent for our cousin. She doesn't seem to be in her room." He was unable to hide the anxiety in his voice.

The King's smile appeared a little devious. "Yes, well, we'll talk about your cousin in a moment. First, let me show you what my men have crafted for your parents." He signaled to the servant next to him, who ran off to fetch the gift. Narfi and Vali shifted their weight uneasily. The absence of Jorda was extremely worrisome. Narfi was beginning to think he had struck a bargain with the sly King too quickly.

One of the craftsmen returned bearing a beautiful wooden casket. He opened it reverently, revealing two delicate golden chalices, one studded with emeralds, the other with sapphires. "We chose emeralds to match your father's eyes, and sapphires for your mother's. Do you approve?" He held the casket out to the boys.

They both peered in, but neither took possession of the chalices. "My Lord, you said you would tell us of our cousin. Please, sir, where is she?"

"Well, she is being prepared, of course, for her wedding," announced Ivaldi.

The jaws of both boys dropped as they stared at the little Dwarf. "Wedding?" cried Vali. "What wedding? She hasn't consented to any wedding!"

The King stood up from his throne and stared hard at the twins. "You are in Svartalfaheim! The only consent that matters here is my own! We made a deal, Asgardian. I may choose as payment anything I feel equal to the value of the chalices, and I choose the hand of Jorda. Now you may take your gifts and go!"

Narfi stood directly in front of the King, his face red with rage. "Jorda is a person, Ivaldi! We cannot offer her as payment for anything! Keep your chalices. We refuse to accept them under these conditions. You tricked us!"

Ivaldi's guards pulled Narfi away. "Trick? I find it most ironic that the sons of Loki would accuse another of tricks! This was your bargain, Narfi Lokison! If you refuse the chalices, then you and your brother will stay and work the mines, and I will still have the lovely Jorda for my bride! Take them below!" commanded Ivaldi, and his men pulled the struggling boys out of the throne room. A muffled cry was heard from the antechamber to the throne room. A tied and gagged Jorda was led roughly to kneel in front of the King. He tore the gag from her mouth so she could speak.

"No, please, I'll marry you, but send them home! Please, Ivaldi, don't punish them so. They'll die in the mines!" she said, beginning to sob.

"So what if they do? They never intended to pay me one dot for all my craftsmen's work. They know full well the price for cheating the royal family of Ivaldi!" he boomed. "I'm having a special crown fashioned for you. Once it is finished, the ceremony shall begin!" He had his guard chain Jorda to his throne. "I don't trust those two, so I'm keeping you close in the meantime, my dear. Please, make yourself comfortable." He leered at her.

* * *

Vali and Narfi were kicked and pushed all the way down into the mines. Here, there was little light save a few dim candles and the air was thick with dust and smoke. Their eyes were streaming from the irritation and they thought they would never stop coughing. They were shackled at the ankles and led to a group of miners who were laboring at the cave walls. Heavy picks were shoved into their hands and they were told to dig. Vali gripped the handle and stared daggers at the Dwarf guards. The guards drew their swords. They outnumbered the boys four to one. Reluctantly, Vali turned to the wall and inflicted his murderous rage upon it.

The boys stripped off their jackets and shirts as they toiled in the sweltering mine. The guards were always nearby and they stopped any conversation among the miners. Their fellow workers consisted of both Dwarves and men. One man set down his pick for but a moment, only to be beaten by the Dwarves. Vali threw his pick at one of the tormentors.. Narfi followed suit, jumping on one of the Dwarves' backs. More guards appeared and they were beaten before being thrown into a dungeon cell. They laid in total darkness on a cold, wet slab of rock. Vali groaned as he crawled towards his brother.

"Narfi?" he called. There was no response. "Narfi, are you okay?" he tried again, but there was still only silence. He reached his brother and put his hand under his head. He felt wetness on Narfi's brow; he feared it was blood. Narfi's chest rose and fell, reassuring Vali that his brother was still alive, but his stillness was terrifying. "Narfi, stay with me, brother. It can't end like this. We're too close; wake up, brother." Vali's voice cracked.

*   *   *

Jorda rested the side of her face against the throne, trying to sleep. Her legs and back ached from sitting still for so long. She noticed a strange ritual performed by King Ivaldi. Every once in a while, usually after the visit from one of his craftsmen, Ivaldi would stand up and face the seat, then turn and sit on his throne again. She worried about her friends, but no one would speak to her. Finally, she put her face in her hands and sobbed.

Down on the floor of the workshop, a Dwarf named Galvi glanced up at the throne. Galvi was young for a Dwarf, not yet so cruel and suspicious as his older brethren. When he saw the maiden called Jorda crying so piteously in her hands, his heart broke. He resolved that he would do what he could to help her.

* * *

Narfi let out a low moan. Vali sat up straight, waiting for another response. "Narfi?" he whispered. "Are you okay?"

"I…don't…" Narfi groaned in pain. "My head…"

"Yes, well, unfortunately, it's still there," Vali quipped. "I'm not too sure about the other bits, however. I can't believe you jumped on that guard's back. Had you thoughts of riding out of Svartalfaheim, my brother?"

There was a small snort from Narfi in reply. "They do rather resemble asses, being all brown and hairy," he said and laughed, before the pain in his ribs stopped him short. "I think they broke a rib or two."

"Narfi, how are we going to get out of this one?" asked a worried Vali.

"Probably in very small pieces," answered Narfi.

* * *

Galvi approached the throne. "Your Majesty, I believe the girl may need to…" he paused, blushing. "To freshen herself, My Lord. May I take her off your hands for a bit?" he asked.

Ivaldi looked at the young Dwarf and nodded his reply. "Take her to the springs, but be quick about it. My heart yearns to have her near me always," he said, leering again. He signaled for his guards to unchain Jorda. She found it difficult to stand, so the little Dwarf came to her side to help her.

"Thank you," she said. Had she been less weary, she might have tried to run, but now she was resigned to her fate. Vali and Narfi were gone and there was nothing she could do.

"My name is Galvi, My Lady. I could not stand to see you so," he said, as they walked towards the underground springs. "How may I help you?"

Jorda looked at the earnest face of the little Dwarf and began to feel the stirrings of hope. "Galvi, why does the King stand and turn at his throne after the craftsmen visit?" she asked.

Galvi looked puzzled for a moment, and then his face brightened as he realized the answer. "That must be when he sends off the artifacts we have made. Sometimes they go to Asgard, sometimes to Alfheim," he explained. "The seat he sits on, it's a magical construct. When he asks it to open, he sends his wares through it to wherever he wishes."

"So it's a passageway, like the passageways of the Elves!" Jorda's face was alight with excitement. "Galvi, when is the King away from his throne?"

Galvi thought for a moment. "Only when he sleeps, My Lady, or when he chooses to eat in the great hall rather than having his meals here. What do you propose?"

"First, I must arrange the rescue of my friends. How can I find them? Ivaldi sent them to the mines. I don't know how long they can last there. Please, Galvi, please help me free them. All we want is to go home."

The Dwarf was beginning to regret his decision to help the Aesir maid. She was asking him to commit an act of treason. He felt sorry for her, but he saw no reason to die for her. "I'm sorry, m'lady, but you ask too much of me. I have no position at court. I have no authority over the guards. There is nothing I can do."

"You can find them and get word to them that I have found a portal. They must not lose hope." She looked thoughtful for a moment. "If I am to be Queen, then I should have a servant. Perhaps I can convince Ivaldi to give me you. You could help me find a way to free my friends from the mines and help us to escape. Perhaps you can create a diversion so the guards aren't watching them. It must be done tonight, while the King sleeps."

Galvi began to sweat. He wrung his hands and paced. "What you ask is madness! No prisoner has ever escaped from Svartalfaheim. And not only that, if I help you, I, too will meet my end, and not in a very nice way, either." He began to tremble.

Jorda raised her head, her eyes closed. "There are animals here. You have ponies to pull the carts, do you not?" she asked, ignoring his protestations.

"Ponies? Y-yes, there are ponies." He knew that she must be mad. He had been fooled by a few tears into helping a madwoman.

"Then there's our diversion. Find out where Vali and Narfi have been taken, and I will send the ponies there to divert the guards. Get them out and bring them here to the throne room." Her eyes shone with hope now. She was sure she had found the way home.

"But what about you, m'lady? Won't the King have you, um, secured? You don't believe he will go to bed and leave you unfettered, do you? And how will you send the ponies? You will be shackled again soon," he said, with genuine regret in his voice.

"I know I can summon them because I can sense them. If I can feel them, I can communicate with them. The King will no doubt lock me in my bedroom tonight. How good are you at picking locks?"

Galvi's face broke into a wide smile. "I am a master locksmith, m'lady. There is no lock I cannot breach," he stated with pride. "Come now, the King will begin to search for you soon. It is late. He will soon be to bed. I will offer my services as your personal guard and release you while he sleeps."

"Dear Galvi. You have given me the finest of all the gifts in Svartalfaheim. You have given me hope," Jorda said.

Galvi took Jorda back to the King's throne and began to replace her chains. "Your Majesty, I have a request," he began, voice trembling. Ivaldi had more than a little drink that evening and was inclined to listen to the little Dwarf. "I would ask Your Majesty to allow me to be the guard of our soon to be Queen. As your wife, she should be afforded all assistance, so that she may better serve you." He bowed so low that his forehead almost touched the floor.

"Yes, a bodyguard for my Queen," Ivaldi said. "Someone to keep her company at all times so that she may not become bored or homesick. It's time for bed. See to it that she is secure in her chambers. I wouldn't want her to fear for her safety while she is here."

"I would beg one more favor of the King," Galvi added. "I would ask for some gold ore, to make a proper crown for Her Highness, and the help of some of the men to carry it back from the mines to the workshop."

Ivaldi gave this some thought. This Dwarf was very ambitious indeed, but he himself had been young once. "So be it," he answered. "Keep up the good work, uh, Gulpy."

"It's Galvi, Your Highness, and thank you most humbly, Sire." He bowed again. He helped Jorda to stand and walked her to her room. A large key protruded from the lock. "We're in luck," he whispered to her. "I will lock the door once you're inside and then slip the key beneath it while no one looks."

Jorda hugged the short little Dwarf, who blushed red. "Thank you, Galvi, with all my heart! The gods will reward you for your kindness."

"My only reward would be that you find a way to keep me blameless in all this. I am now your sworn keeper. Your disappearance will be on my head!" he said, his voice a whimper.

"Not if you were overcome by two strong young Asgardian men, left beaten in your brave attempt to prevent my abduction," she suggested.

Galvi flinched at the word "beaten." "We'll see when the time comes, m'lady. For now, I must be off to the mines. Pray that I may find your friends."

*   *   *

Galvi crept carefully along the steep passages and steps leading down into the mines. He had assumed the new prisoners would be working the gold mines. Gold was by far the favorite metal of the Dwarves and they were in constant need of it. When he came to the entrance to the mine, he found several guards missing. "I have come at the behest of the King. I am to retrieve gold ore to make a crown for our Queen. It is his command that some of you help me, but I see that you are shorthanded. Where are the others?" he inquired.

"They've gone to fetch two of the slaves who misbehaved," sneered one of the guards.

"They've been cooling their heels in the dungeon. The one was badly hurt. He'll be food for the ponies tonight, I expect," laughed another.

"Help me load the hod and fetch some ponies. Once the others have returned, we will take the ore to the forges," Galvi commanded.

The guards didn't like the little Dwarf's arrogance, but they knew better than to cross the King. They obeyed, pushing a cart over to a pile of mined gold ore and began loading the heavy mineral into it.

*   *   *

A small light began to glow behind a peephole in the door of the cell that held Vali and Narfi. A key was placed in the lock and a guard, assisted by seven others, waited at the door. "Time to go back to work," snarled the guard.

Vali was about to protest when Narfi stopped him. "Good news, indeed. This job has done wonders for my pecs," he said. He stood straight, ignoring the stabbing pain in his side.

"And the biceps," added Vali.

"We'll be big as Thor by week's end," said Narfi.

The guards shoved them into the corridor and marched them back to the mine. As they neared, they noticed a small Dwarf hitching a pony to a cart. "Is that you, Galvi?" asked the guard. "Are you working in the shop now?"

Galvi spotted the boys and gave a little gasp at their bruised and torn bodies. "W-what happened to them?" he queried, voice shaking.

"What do you mean, worker? I see nothing wrong with these slaves. Now go about your business, and let them go back to work," snapped the guard.

"I can't seem to get these straps done right. Please, I've never hitched up a cart before," Galvi lied. Grudgingly, the guards took over the cart and pony duties. Galvi found his opportunity and whispered to Narfi, "Take heart. Your friend has a plan. It involves ponies." He dropped the key to their chains into Vali's hand just as the guards turned to hand Galvi the pony's lead.

"Thanks," Galvi said to the guard. "Now, if you would be so kind as to escort me back to the workshop," he commanded.

"Why should we escort you, little worker?" asked the guard.

"Because I shall need your help emptying the ore into the forge, and because the King told me to get your help," Galvi said.

The guards looked at one another and with a shrug and four of them left with Galvi. The six guards left behind walked back to the entrance of the mine, leaving the prisoners alone to do their work. Suddenly, there was a slight trembling felt under foot. Vali quickly unlocked his and Narfi's ankle chains and passed the key to the other prisoners. The sound of low rumbling began to grow until it was as loud as thunder. With earsplitting whinnies and shrieks, forty or fifty ponies stampeded towards the guards. Unable to reach the large open area of the mine in time, the guards were crushed beneath the ponies' hooves. The small horses stopped short as they entered the mine. They stood calmly, as if waiting for further instruction.

"Narfi, this is Jorda's doing. We should climb on their backs and keeping low, ride out of here!" Addressing the other miners, he said, "Mount your horses, men! Tonight, we escape the mines of Svartalfaheim!" With a shout, the men jumped aboard the ponies and galloped up the passages towards freedom.

When he met up with Galvi and the other guards, Vali swung his pick and easily took out three of them before the others took off in fright. Galvi trembled in front of him, arms shielding his head. "You needn't fear, friend. I know you are the one who brought word to us from Jorda. Climb on with me, and I will take you up with us."

"No!" shouted Galvi. "I cannot be seen aiding you in any way! You must strike me down, so the King will believe I had nothing to do with this!" He lowered his arms and shut his eyes tight, bravely waiting for the first blow.

"You show great courage, my friend. I will do my best to do you as little harm as possible." With that, Vali backhanded the little Dwarf to the ground. "Are you alright?" he asked, offering a hand to help him up again.

Galvi smiled weakly, tasting blood in his mouth.

"I've been better," he said, laughing, "but I've been worse, too. The Lady Jorda waits for you in the throne room, but there were two of you, were there not?" Galvi searched the passage for signs of the Asgardian's brother.

In the turmoil of the escape, Vali had not thought to keep an eye on Narfi. With growing alarm, he turned back to search for his brother. He found him bent double, one shoulder propping him against the wall of the mine. "Narfi, I'm here! We must take the ponies to the throne room before the guards come to their senses and warn the others!"

Narfi did not move, just leaned against the wall, gasping for air. "Fell…horse…tripped," he wheezed, in obvious pain. "Landed…on…ribs." He stopped to cough up some blood. "Lung…punctured. Can't …breathe…" With that, he collapsed.

Half crazed, Vali searched the mine for something to help his brother. He spied one of the empty hods nearby and lifted his brother into it. "Galvi, help me hitch the ponies. We must get Narfi to the portal. Quickly!"

Without hesitation, Galvi swiftly hitched two stout ponies to the crate and slapped them into a trot. He and Vali sped their pace by pushing from behind. They passed the bodies of the other guards, apparently slain by the angry miners. Finally, they came to the entrance to the throne room. Vali lifted his brother's limp body onto his shoulder. "You must go now, Galvi. Someday I swear, we will find a way to repay you," he promised.

"There is no need, my friend. I have never had such an adventure! Now, get you to the throne. It will take you where you need be." He extended his hand, which Vali shook.

Vali was so determined to save his brother that his weight was inconsequential. He ran to Jorda, who had begun to run towards him. Her face was streaked with tears as she looked at the state of the twins. "Is he, is he…" She could not finish her sentence.

"No, he is not dead, not yet. He has suffered a punctured lung. We must get to the room and then to Vanaheim for help as quickly as possible," he urged. They faced the throne. Jorda spoke to it, saying, "We wish to return to Asgard." She turned to Vali as the seat vanished, revealing a reddish glow. "I'll go first and open the door to Vanaheim so that you can rush him through as soon as you arrive."

"Yes, go. I'll be right behind," he promised. Jorda climbed feet first through the seat and was gone. Vali carefully maneuvered himself and his brother through the opening, and they, too, vanished.

CHAPTER 7

Narfi began to wake, but wasn't sure he should open his eyes yet. He could feel bandages around his chest and head. He also detected soft pillows and silken sheets. There was the scent of lilacs as he took a tentative breath and was delighted to find that he could in fact breathe deeply again. With some apprehension, he cracked open his eyelids and surveyed his room. One wall was made of floor to ceiling windows which had been opened to let in the fragrant summer air. Large vases filled with flowers sat on practically every surface. Ornately embroidered cushions adorned chairs and couches about the room. He knew where he was--the palace of Freya, the Empress of Vanaheim. Freya was the goddess of love and beauty and surrounded herself with only the most beautiful things.

Narfi tried to sit himself up but found that he was still weak. To his right, a young handmaiden rushed to his side.

"You must rest, my lord," she admonished. "You were at death's door when you entered our realm."

"Where are my brother and cousin?" he asked. "Are they alright? I don't remember anything after the mine." Even this small effort to speak exhausted him.

"Quiet, my lord. The lady Freya will be most happy to learn that you are awake at last," she said, beaming. She plumped his pillow and rearranged his covers before leaving to inform her mistress of the good news. Within moments, the goddess herself sat on the edge of Narfi's bed.

She gently brushed the hair from his eyes. "Poor boy, you have suffered such grave injuries. You are very strong indeed to have overcome them."

With the touch of Freya's fingers, Narfi felt his anxiety wash away. He had wanted to ask her something…what was it again? "Lady Freya," he began. "I wanted to know…that is, I needed to ask…" His voice faded and he was unable to recall his question.

"There, there, my boy. You must drink. You have been asleep for days. Here, drink this." She offered him a crystal goblet of golden nectar. "You will feel better soon." She smiled benignly then leaned close and kissed his forehead, lingering long enough for Narfi to glance down at her perfect bosom. He blushed slightly and looked away. Her lips parted, and her fingertips caressed his face. "Rest, Narfi Lokison. We must build up your strength now, mustn't we?" She stood, her eyes dreamy as she gazed at the boy.

Narfi was thoroughly embarrassed by the stirrings he felt in the pit of his stomach and lower. Though Freya's age was timeless, Narfi had always thought of her as a contemporary of his mother and father. He knew their age difference was vast, but she was still the most beautiful woman in all of the nine realms, and he wanted her. He was confused and a little frightened by these feelings and tried to place his thoughts elsewhere. There was something he needed to do, if only he could remember.

* * *

As soon as Vali and Jorda had entered Vanaheim with the unconscious Narfi between them, they had called for help. A group of the Vani had heard their cries and rushed to their aid. Narfi was carried to the palace while Vali and Jorda were taken to the local councilman's chambers. The councilman, named Ragnvaldr, kept them waiting for hours. Finally, he had them escorted to their rooms to clean themselves and to rest. They gratefully accepted the rooms and the baths and both fell asleep within minutes of lying across their beds.

The next morning, they found a sumptuous breakfast waiting for them in their rooms. After eating to their fill, they tried their doors only to find them locked. They called out, but no one came. By shouting they were able to hear each other, their rooms being situated across from each other.

"Vali, what do you think is going on?" Jorda wondered.

"I don't know. Perhaps it's just a precaution. I thought we were getting closer to the present with each door, but maybe we're back during the war with Asgard again," Vali replied.

"What do you think they've done with Narfi?" Jorda's voice began to rise, panic threatening to take hold.

"Don't worry," Vali shouted in reply. "This is Vanaheim. They have healers every bit as talented as those in Asgard. I'm sure he is being well cared for." He was trying to reassure himself as much as his cousin Jorda.

"I hope you're right," Jorda answered. She then began to explore her room. She tested the large window overlooking the rose garden and found it sealed tight, the glass unbreakable. The fireplace was a magical construct, and had no flue. She was trapped within another prison, albeit a much more pleasant one. She heard a key in the lock and a handmaiden entered to take the breakfast things away.

"Please, my cousin Vali and I arrived bearing my injured cousin Narfi. Could you please tell me how he is? Can we see him?" Jorda asked.

The girl looked puzzled. "I know not of whom you speak, my lady. There were only two," she said.

Jorda's heart sank. She was not mad; she knew what had transpired. This servant girl's attempt to convince her that Narfi never returned with them was disturbing. Why the deception? "Why am I locked in this room? When may I see my cousin Vali?"

"I'm afraid I cannot answer you, madam. My duties are with you and no other." The maid approached a large cupboard standing against one wall. "The Lady Freya has provided fresh clothing for you, madam. I believe she will see you at supper." She opened wide the doors to reveal dozens of expertly crafted gowns, shoes, and billowy undergarments. "She prefers that her guests dress appropriately for supper. I suggest the indigo velvet gown." She hung the dress on a hook inside the door. "I will call for you at eight." Having completed her duties, the maid left with the tray of breakfast dishes.

Once sure the girl was gone, Jorda called out to her cousin again. "Vali, the servant girl says I'm to dine with Freya tonight. Have you the same invitation?"

"No. I'm to dine with the councilman. Perhaps we'll get some answers tonight. Don't lose heart. I'm sure things will be sorted out before tomorrow," Vali assured her.

The two were visited by various servants throughout the day. Some brought food, others cleaned and refreshed their rooms. None brought information. That evening, near supper time, Jorda was attended by Freya's handmaiden who helped her to dress for the formal occasion. As a citizen of Alfheim, Jorda was dressed first in an indigo gown, covered by a pale blue lambskin vest that reached to within inches of the hem of her dress. Her blond hair was bound up and decorated with matching blue ribbons and flowers. The maid fussed and primped until she was at last content that the girl's appearance would please her mistress.

Vali was attended by Ragnvaldr's manservant who helped the young Asgardian into the dress uniform of his Realm, which consisted of leather, multiple straps, and traditional symbols arranged here and there according to Asgardian ceremony.

Jorda and Vali were escorted from their rooms at the same moment, and both were impressed by the other's appearance in spite of themselves. "You look..." Vali hunted for the right word. "Stunning," he said.

Blushing, Jorda replied, "And you, My Lord." They tried to approach one another but were escorted away to their appointed destinations.

*   *   *

Ragnvaldr's home was an imposing castle composed entirely of polished black marble. Vali and his party of the councilman's servants entered the courtyard by carriage. Vali was shown into a dining hall--large but still small enough for more intimate dinners, rather than the gala feasts prepared for affairs of state. Ragnvaldr sat at the head of the table while Vali was seated at its opposite. They exchanged polite salutations, and the councilman motioned for his staff to serve supper.

"Sir, your hospitality is most graciously appreciated," began Vali, "but one must wonder about the hospitality of keeping one's guests locked in one's rooms. I fear I must ask you, sir, what would you have of us? I would also ask of you the keeping place and condition of my brother." Though he kept his voice even and without emotion, Vali's eyes were hard.

Ragnvaldr narrowed his eyes as he stared at the boy. "I am not sure I like the tone of your questions, Master Vali Lokison." His eyes softened as he continued. "However, you are your father's son, and Loki has never been a man known for his tact. To answer your question, you have been kept locked in your rooms for your own protection. Although there is a truce between our Realms, there are still those who feel that Vanaheim was slighted in the exchange that brought peace to our nations. My fellow leaders and I are content, but I felt compelled to protect you, none the less. I meant no disrespect."

"You still have not told me the fate of my brother. I demand to see him," insisted Vali.

The councilman sat back and studied Vali for a while before answering. "Your brother is healing well in Freya's palace. I'm afraid that his wounds will require more time before he can receive visitors. He is weak, and his heart is delicate. It would not be in his best interest to have visitors at this time."

Vali's eyes never left Ragnvaldr's. He knew deceit when he saw it. What he couldn't understand was the reason for it. They were not enemies of Vanaheim. None of the Vani that had helped carry Narfi to safety had seemed in the least bit suspicious or angry. This all had a personal feel to it, and Vali could not for the life of him understand why. "We wish you no harm, Councilman Ragnvaldr. We only wish to return to Asgard. I would in no way disturb my brother's recovery. I only ask to see him for myself so that I may be at peace. The last I saw of him, he looked near death. Surely you can't deny me..." Vali was stopped mid-sentence.

"Of course I can deny you, son of Loki! You are our guest here. Who do you think you are that you can make demands on me? I have spoken to the Empress Freya, and we both agree that you and your cousin shall be returned to Asgard, but your brother must remain until such time he is whole again." Servants brought plates of food and flagons of drink. "Now, let us speak no more of it. Enjoy your supper," the councilman said.

Vali pushed himself from the table and stood. "I'm afraid I have no appetite, sir. I beg that you pardon me, and see to it that I am returned to my room." Nostrils flaring, Vali clenched his fists as he stared down at the prominent citizen of Vanaheim.

Ragnvaldr's smile was cold. He turned to one of his servants and commanded, "See that young Vali is returned to his quarters. He has lost his appetite."

Vali was escorted back to the main entrance where he waited for the coach to draw near. For some reason, the leaders of Vanaheim had decided to take Narfi hostage. He was beside himself with both anger and anxiety. He paced until the arrival of the coach and stomped heavily on board. Once seated and riding swiftly away from Ragnvaldr's castle, his mind turned to thoughts of Jorda. He hoped her evening with Freya was more rewarding.

* * *

Jorda was escorted into a cozy parlor with a small round table already set with plates of food. Freya greeted her with warmth at the door and led her to her chair. "Thank you, My Lady," Jorda said, with a curtsey. "You are very kind to invite me to your home."

Freya's smile was radiant. "My dear, you needn't be so formal. I've had them prepare a light repast so we could sit and talk at leisure. The Alfheim are always welcome here in Vanaheim," she said.

"Of course, we are sister Realms. My mother, Jord, has always enjoyed her visits here, but of course, she has never been to court," Jorda replied sheepishly.

"I have met your mother. She was invaluable in helping us control a vicious pack of wolves that had threatened our community. Are you so talented as she?" Freya offered Jorda some tea.

"Not yet, My Lady, but I hope to be one day." Jorda was nervous as she sipped her tea. She was running out of small talk and had no idea what to say. She had never dined with an Empress before. She set down her teacup and placed a white linen napkin on her lap. "Forgive me for asking, My Lady, but my cousin Vali and I are concerned for Narfi. He was so badly hurt when we last saw him. Could we please be taken to him?"

Freya made a clucking sound against her teeth. "Oh, my dear, Narfi is still much too ill to have visitors at this time. But be reassured, he is on the mend. I will fetch you myself the moment he is ready." She sliced a bit of food and brought it to her lips. "You must try the pheasant, dear Jorda. My cooks are the best in all the Realms."

Jorda stared down at her food but had no desire to eat. "I'm sorry, My Lady, but you have fed us so well already. I'm afraid that I cannot eat a bite." She pushed the plate away from her and folded her hands in her lap.

Freya put down her fork and looked at Jorda with an exaggerated frown. "Oh, too bad. I hoped to give you a proper send off before your trip back to Asgard tomorrow. I suppose we'll have to make you a basket of cold meat and fruits for you to take with you. We will send your cousin Narfi to you when he is better, if he is so inclined."

"What do you mean, 'so inclined?'" asked Jorda with some alarm.

"The few times young Narfi has spoken to me, he seemed quite content to remain here in the palace. I dare say the boy is a bit infatuated with me, but there you have it." She stood and nodded to a servant. "Take Jorda back to her quarters, and see to it that she stays there until morning. She and her cousin Vali shall be returned to Asgard immediately after breakfast." She nodded at Jorda and was gone.

*   *   *

Narfi sat at a little table in his room. He wore silk pajamas and a heavy velvet dressing gown. When he first sat down to eat, he had thought himself ravenous, but suddenly felt disinclined to consume even one bite. He stood up slowly, his sides and back still sore from the beating he took-- when? There had been some altercation. He had been beaten but where? "I must have taken a few blows to my head," he mumbled to himself. "I think… I think there was a horse, perhaps. Yes, I must have fallen from my horse. That explains the bruises," he continued, still thinking out loud.

Freya entered and strode across the room to stand behind Narfi. She placed her hands on his shoulders and began to massage his neck. "Your bruises are fading, dear lad. Look here." She opened his shirt and passed her hands over his chest. "Hardly a mark at all."

Narfi closed his eyes and allowed Freya to caress him. Narfi had never given much thought about the fair sex. At that particular moment, however, he couldn't understand why he had not. Freya's touch was exquisite. He laid his head back, eyes still closed, in abject pleasure. The next thing he knew, her mouth was on his. He did not protest; on the contrary, he kissed her back, drinking in the softness of her lips and skin and her intoxicating scent. Before he knew it, she had maneuvered him next to the bed.

"Tonight, lesson one," she said, smiling as she slipped his clothing to the floor.

*   *   *

Vali and Jorda caught a quick glimpse of one another as they were shown back into their rooms. As soon as their escorts had left, they began to talk to one another through their respective doors. "They're sending us back!" cried Vali.

"Yes, I know," answered Jorda. "They refused to let either of us go to Narfi. Why, Vali? Why do they want Narfi? Why not send all of us back?"

"I don't know," said Vali, "and I don't see that there's anything we can do. Except…" He paused, an idea dawning in his head. "We'll let them send us to Asgard, but you know where we'll wind up. Once in the room, we'll sneak back into Vanaheim, find Narfi, and figure out a way back again."

"That doesn't sound like a very good plan, Vali. How are we supposed to find Narfi? How are we supposed to get out of Vanaheim?"

"We'll do what we always have. We'll wing it," laughed Vali.

"Wing it? That's the best you can do?" she asked, incredulous. "Wing it? You are mad."

"Have you a better plan?" Vali asked.

"No," admitted Jorda. "I guess that's our best bet, then. We should probably get some rest. I want to be bright eyed and clear headed tomorrow." She stood up from where she had been sitting in front of the door. "Good night, Vali."

"Yeah, sure, sleep," agreed Vali. He was sure he wouldn't sleep a wink but told himself at least to try. "Good night, Jorda." He was about to go to his bed when he stopped, turning back to face the door. "Jorda?" he asked.

"Yes," she answered.

Vali hesitated for a moment before saying, "I'm really sorry about all of this. Narfi and I, we should never have gotten you involved."

Jorda smiled as she leaned her head and hands against the door. "What? And miss all this?" she said and laughed. Vali gave a little laugh himself, and the two went off to their separate beds.

Early the next morning, servants bustled noisily into the friend's rooms, waking them. Neither had slept well and they greeted each other bleary eyed and disheveled. They were hurried into their baths where they bathed and dressed. By the time they were ready, Freya and Ragnvaldr had arrived in the corridor to see them off. The four of them, accompanied by half a dozen of Freya's biggest and strongest guards, walked down the wide hallway to the tall doors that led out. A coach waited for them beyond the door and next to the door of the coach, stood Narfi.

Vali's and Jorda's eyes lit up when they saw Narfi, standing tall and looking good as new. Better, in fact; he was dressed in the finest attire Vanaheim afforded its young men. He was polished and well groomed and looked a bit bored with the whole situation. "Narfi! By the gods! We thought you might be dead!" shouted Vali as he ran towards his brother. Narfi stepped back in alarm.

"Guards!" Narfi shouted, and indicated they should grab this upstart who dared to approach him uninvited.

Jorda's face turned from delight to utter astonishment. "Narfi, what are you doing?" she asked. "You're coming with us, aren't you? That's why you're here, isn't it?"

"Freya informs me that there is a fellow here who claims to be my brother, and a girl who claims to be my cousin. I came down here to face you both, and to tell you that your foolish attempt at deception has failed. I do not know either of you, and suggest you go on your merry way at once, and leave me and my friends alone!" Narfi turned his back to them, mounted his horse, and turned to face them one last time. "I don't know what your game is, but it is plain to see that my place is here, in Vanaheim, with my Queen." He glanced in Freya's direction, a loving smile crossing his face. And then, with a swift kick, he was gone.

Vali and Jorda stared at each other, mouths wide in shock. Freya addressed them, "I told you he has no inclination to leave. Narfi stays here, with me. You, on the other hand, shall be escorted to the portal of Asgard." She clapped her hands and guards pushed the two dejected cousins into the carriage. Neither spoke a word throughout the ride or as they were walked to the portal entrance. With a loud crack and bright flash of light, they found themselves back in the chamber of doors, minus Narfi.

Vali ran to the door they had just exited and yanked it open. Instead of the fields of Vanaheim lying in front of him, there was solid rock. He yanked open the door next to it, and the one after that, but they were all set against hard cave walls. Through all of this, he had been strong. He had vowed not to get discouraged, even to try to bolster the spirits of his companions, but this was too much. He sank to his knees and let the tears flow. He bent until his face was pressed against his fists on the floor. A piteous wail came from the deepest part of his soul as he confronted the loss of his brother.

Jorda, her own face stained with tears, crouched next to him, cradling him. "Vali, there is still Asgard. The last door. Come on now; we must go through it," she coaxed.

Vali sat up, took a few deep breaths, and wiped his face on his sleeve. They hugged each other, friend to friend, and helped one another stand. "Jorda," he began, straining not to start sobbing again. "I don't think... I can't..." His words failed him.

"Yes, you can, Vali. We'll go back to Asgard and we'll find a way to get him back. Remember, you are Loki's son."

Vali turned tortured eyes upon her, but managed a weak smile. "Yes, I am Loki's son, and I am not ready to give up, yet." He took her hand, and approached the final door.

* * *

Loki's apprehension was growing. Although it still had not been a full day that the children were gone, he felt a gnawing unease in his gut. When he spied three riderless horses returning from the wood, his heart sank. He immediately gathered Sigyn and Thor to form a manhunt and sent word to Jorda's mother, the goddess Jord. Jord arrived almost immediately. They proposed to ride into the forest, and Jord asked for Jorda's mount from that day. Skaldra was brought to her. She stroked the horse's nose and spoke softly to her before swinging herself into the saddle. Loki retold the story the twins had told to him about a cave in the forest, and about the portal. Thor, Sigyn, and Loki all thought they knew where the cave was from Narfi's description. Jord said Skaldra knew exactly where they stopped and the four of them ran as fast as their horses could carry them into the wood.

They came to the entrance to the cave the boys had discovered. With a flick of his wrist, Loki lit the cave as bright as day. Thor smashed the entryway with his hammer, making it large enough for all to enter. They slid into the cavern and felt along its walls, hoping to find the portal. Sigyn listened carefully as she crept along the wide passageway and then came to a stop, her head turning left towards the rock wall. "I hear something," she whispered. "I think I hear Vali's voice."

At that moment, a rectangular sort of nothingness appeared in the wall, and a door opened. Jorda stepped through, followed closely by Vali. Sigyn and Jord rushed to and smothered their children in their arms. Loki turned troubled eyes toward Thor. Then he grabbed up his son and after a quick but crushing embrace, he held him at arm's length. "Vali, where's Narfi?"

Vali looked miserable. Lips trembling, he said, "We had to leave him, Father. Freya and Ragnvaldr had us forced into the portal. Narfi could have come with us, but he refused. He didn't even recognize us!"

Thor caught the murderous look in his brother's eye. "Loki, don't make things worse. Freya is loved by everyone in all the nine realms. If you were to harm her, I could not stop what would happen next. You would be banished at best, torn limb from limb at worst."

"You can't go to Vanaheim to get Narfi, Loki," said Jorda. Vali stepped to her side. "We left the cave and entered a room of nine doors, one door for each Realm. We never knew where or when we were going," she tried to explain.

Vali spoke next. "We arrived in Midgard aboard the Titanic just as it hit the iceberg, back in Earth year 1912. Then we entered Alfheim back in the days of the war between Vanaheim and Asgard, and so on, for each Realm. Fenrir helped us escape Jotunheim, and offered to contact you if he arrived in Asgard without us."

Loki's face registered surprise. "You met Fenrir?" he asked.

"Oh, yes, and Hela, and Angrboda. It's alright Father, we know all about it. Angrboda was very kind, as was Fenrir. Narfi and I promised to visit…" Vali stopped short. He remembered that there may be no more 'Narfi and I.' He hung his head and turned away.

Jorda placed a hand on Vali's shoulder and continued to explain. "Narfi warned us that the portals operated on their own time scale. If we were in Jotunheim in what was the past in Asgard time, trying to confront someone in the present could upset the balance of nature. It would interfere with the space-time continuum or something like that."

Loki thought this over for a moment. "Vali, where did you get these garments?" he asked.

"They're from Vanaheim, Father. Freya gave them to me. Our other clothes were, well, sort of tattered from the mines of Svartalfheim," Vali said.

"The mines!" shouted Sigyn. She rushed to her son and grabbed him to her again. "Oh, my dear, brave Vali! I can't bear it! The mines!" She clutched his face in her hands, staring into his eyes. "Thank the gods you made it home. Don't worry, my sweet. Your father will find a way. We will find your brother and bring him home as well. You'll see." She smiled at her son.

"Give me your vest," instructed Loki. Vali handed over the leather garment, which Loki examined carefully. He ran his hands along the seams and held it close to his face, breathing in the scent of the leather and dye used to color it. "This was recently fashioned. It can't be more than three months old. It is my opinion you arrived at Vanaheim in the near present. There should be no disturbance in the space-time continuum, though for a sorcerer, that should not be an issue, anyway." He looked to the others. "I should go to Vanaheim alone. If it is safe, I will send for you."

Thor protested, "On what pretense will you go to Vanaheim? Do you think Freya will hand over your son simply because you ask? She has some purpose in all of this. As King of Asgard, she must obey me."

"Unless her purpose is to incite a new war between the Vani and the Asgardians," said Jord. "If she has worked some spell on Narfi causing him to be bound to her, he will refuse to leave. If you were to force him, there may be violence and the beginnings of what could become war." The others stared incredulously at her. "Believe me, I understand conflict and discord. This feels like a plan to induce war."

Sigyn grabbed Loki's arm. "Can you reverse such a spell? Can you convince our son to come home willingly? Loki, what are we going to do?" Her tears had dried. She believed in her husband and had faith that he would put things right.

Loki stared into his wife's anxious face. "Well, there's only one way to find out, isn't there?" With that, he vanished.

* * *

Narfi lay on his back, his hands behind his head. "I hope I was able to please you, my Queen?" he asked.

Freya stood naked beside the bed. "You have become quite inventive, young lord," she answered. "You please me very well. Are you happy here?" she asked him.

"Most happy, my Queen! I would stay with you forever, if it could be so."

The Empress leaned across the bed and kissed Narfi's cheek. "It shall be. We must not let anyone come between us, then. Not anyone, ever." Narfi smiled and reached for her but she stood, turning to replace her clothing. "Not now, my dearest. I must attend matters of state." She gave him a coy smile. "But I have friends who wish to visit you. It would please your Queen if you would entertain them."

Narfi looked uncomfortable, remembering the last visit of Freya's friends. "Let me come with you. Please, my Queen. I live only to serve you," he begged.

Freya looked down at him with an evil grin. "Yes, I know, dear Narfi Lokison, but do not despair. Only death shall ever part us."

* * *

Thor and the others stared at the spot where a moment ago Loki had stood. "My brother, I hope you know what you're doing," Thor muttered. "We must go to Vanaheim. Freya must be stopped. Somehow, we must maintain peace between our Realms. We can't sit idly by and allow her to carry out her plans," he stated.

"There is little I can do to help in Vanaheim," said Sigyn. "They are immune to my song. I will stay here with the children. Thor, you must trust Loki. He has probably formulated a plan and worked out every contingency. If you go, follow his lead. He will bring my Narfi home, and save us from war. I believe in him."

Thor smiled down at his sister-in-law. "If you tell this to my brother, I will deny it," he said, "but I was always jealous of Loki when I saw the two of you together. I never had anyone look at me with such complete and utter love, requiring no more from one another than just to be in each other's company. If you say to trust him, then I will. That's not to say we shouldn't say a prayer or two, however!" He laughed.

"Daily, my brother," she said, laughing also, before she sobered. "Now, go, and save my child." She reached up and kissed him on his cheek.

*   *   *

Loki had materialized in Freya's bedchamber in the form of a fly. He watched as Freya left the bed she had shared with his son and overheard the subsequent conversation. She seemed to have him bound to her by a simple love spell, but Loki knew there had to be something more to cause Narfi to deny his family and his homeland. Loki remembered the spell that Sigyn had placed on her former husband to facilitate his and Sigyn's continued love affair. The spell had been broken by the shock of Fingardin seeing Loki's twin sons, for all the world looking like younger versions of their father, standing in front of him at the palace of Asgard. Perhaps if he could find a way to shock Narfi into seeing how little Freya actually cared for him, he might break or at least weaken the hold she had on him. One way would be to show Freya in the throes of passion with another man; a bigger shock would be if the other man was Narfi's own father. Freya had tried to seduce Loki once. She had hated him ever since when he had laughed at her efforts. Now that she had his son, perhaps Freya would be so arrogant as to believe she could have the father.

He flew away in search of Freya. He found her in the Council chambers, conferring with Ragnvaldr. The councilman was speaking. "Thor and Jord have arrived, My Lady. The children must have returned to Asgard and related their story. Are you sure Narfi will deny them as well?" he asked.

"What of Loki? Was he not with them?" Freya asked.

"No, My Lady. I suspect that he probably preceded them in disguise. You perceived that he would be the most likely to thwart your chances at success. Thor is the King of Asgard. You must receive him," the councilman said.

"Of course. Bring me young Lokison. Let them hear for themselves his commitment to me and to Vanaheim. Thor is hotheaded enough to try to kidnap him on the spot. Naturally, Narfi will fight him. Such violence will only escalate. Poor Narfi could easily lose his life in the battle, along with several Vani. War would be inevitable, and this time, Asgard would fall under the rule of Frey and Freya, as it should have always been."

Ragnvaldr bowed and left to honor her command.

The moment Ragnvaldr was gone, Loki appeared before Freya. "It is not enough that you take my son to your bed, you will see him murdered as well?" he asked. "Tell me, Freya, does this have anything to do with you and me?" He came within touching distance of the Queen.

Freya looked through narrowed eyes at the face of Loki. "I can't tell you how fortunate it was the day your little bastards arrived here in Vanaheim, Loki. Narfi was near death. I considered just letting him die, but then I thought of a better use for him. He is about the age you were, when I came to you. It is almost as if I have had you, after all. You were more experienced, of course, having been rutting around with that little farmer's daughter, Sigyn." She stepped back, a cruel smile on her face.

Loki smiled and came within a breath of her. He slid a finger along Freya's face and jaw. "I am even more experienced now," he whispered. "I suggest an exchange.

Send Narfi back to his mother, and I will stay here with you. I have no care who sits at the top of Yggdrasil. Whether Vanaheim or Asgard rule means nothing to me. If it's power you want, you know that I can help you attain it." He tipped her chin up towards him and kissed her. He pulled her body against his and kissed more deeply.

Freya's first reaction was to resist, but as Loki held her and kissed her, she began to respond with equal passion of her own. She threw her arms around him, and they stood in tight embrace. It was at that moment that Ragnvaldr returned with Narfi, followed by the escorted Thor and Jord.

All stood in silent shock as Loki and Freya continued to kiss. It wasn't until Thor noisily cleared his throat that they broke apart.

Jord closed her eyes for a moment, scarcely breathing. When she opened her eyes again, there were small flames within them.

Narfi's face reddened with rage. "What is this? Freya? Father? What…" He stopped and drew his dagger.

Ragnvaldr drew his sword, but was knocked aside by Thor. "Narfi!" Thor shouted. "Think what you're about to do! Stop, and think!"

Jord's influence had raised passions in the room to near frenzy. Freya clung to Loki, smiling coyly at Narfi. Thor readied himself to strike dead any who approached him. Narfi fell to his knees in anguish.

"Narfi," Jord whispered, "remember who you are. You are Loki's son. You are the son of the god of Mischief. Remember that, and be free."

Narfi's shoulders began to relax as realization began to dawn on him. The spell was broken. His father had seen to it. Freya had deceived him by giving him potions and seducing him with her powers as the goddess of love. He remembered sending away his brother and cousin. Now he was beside himself with shame and remorse. "Father…" he called, voice trembling.

Loki pushed Freya to the ground and ran to embrace his son. "I'm sorry, Narfi. I had to try to bring you out of the spell. I'm so sorry for the hurt it caused you." He held his son tightly to his chest.

"No, Father, I let you down. I let everyone down. I allowed her to deceive me. I'm the one who is sorry, Father. So sorry." Narfi's voice broke into sobs.

Jord whispered to Thor. "We are done here. You needn't raise your hammer. It is time to leave." Thor visibly relaxed and allowed his arms to drop to his sides. To Ragnvaldr, she whispered, "Freya has proven herself an unworthy ruler. She has used her petty jealousy and need for revenge to bring you to the brink of war. She should be deposed." Ragnvaldr stood and glared at Freya.

To Freya, she said, "Your council is against you. They threaten to overthrow you and usurp your power. They must be punished severely." Freya screamed for her guards and demanded they take Ragnvaldr to prison for interrogation. Jord's eyes returned to normal.

Loki, Narfi, Thor, and Jord watched the growing chaos and then calmly left the chamber to return to Asgard.

CHAPTER 8

Sigyn, Vali, and Jorda waited at Heimdall's post on the edge of the Bifrost. Vali paced while Jorda wrung her hands.

"Patience, my dears," Sigyn said. "They will return soon. It will all be fine once again. Just wait and see." She gave each a pat on the shoulder and smiled into the Bifrost, waiting the return of her beloved Loki and the others.

Heimdall responded to a command he alone could hear, placed the sword key into its lock, and brought the heroes home. Sigyn allowed Vali to be the first to run and throw his arms around his brother.

"I'm so sorry, Vali," Narfi said. "It's no wonder Freya picked me. She knew you would be much too strong to fall for her deceits." He tuned his tortured face towards his brother, his eyes brimming.

"Don't be an idiot, Narfi. She picked you because you were half dead, and she still had to drug you and use all her powers to get you," Vali replied.

Loki pulled his wife to him, and they kissed. "I had to be a bit, um, creative, with Freya. I had to do something to shock Narfi out of it, so I…"

Sigyn put her fingers to his lips. "I trust you, Loki. You needn't share every detail. You brought our son back home to us. That is all that matters." She gave him another hug and then pulled Narfi to her. "Are you alright, my love?" she asked.

Narfi sighed deeply as he laid his head against her shoulder. "It's been rather a rough few months, Mother, but I think I'll get better in time," he replied.

Thor offered his arm to Jord. "Very clever, Jord. I believe that thanks to you, the only war in our future may be a civil one, amongst the hierarchy of Vanaheim."

Jorda slipped her arm around her mother's waist on her side opposite Thor. "Mother, I think I may want to stay here in Asgard for a while longer. I still want to come home for visits, and you will come here to see me, won't you?" she asked.

"That sounds like a splendid idea, my daughter, but your cousin Loki and I must not stay in close vicinity of one another for very long. Disastrous things can occur when the god of Chaos and the goddess of Discord remain in each other's company for any length of time. Isn't that right, cousin?" she addressed Loki.

"Yes, I seem to recall a vacation we once took to some British colonies on Earth during their eighteenth century. It resulted in a Revolution, did it not?" asked Loki.

"You had to befriend that tall, red-haired, Virginia farmer, didn't you? Named Jefferson, wasn't he?" asked Jord.

"Your little excursion up to Boston wasn't without incident, Jord. They held a sort of tea party, I believe. Threw all that perfectly good tea into the harbor, did they not?" smiled Loki.

Jorda and the twins rolled their eyes. "Old people and their reminisces," she teased.

Vali and Narfi raised their fists to one another and bumped them together. "Where's that ox you were going to eat when we got back?" Narfi quizzed Vali.

"That's a good question, brother. I think I should like to visit the kitchens," Vali announced.

"That sounds good to me," agreed Jorda.

"To the kitchens!" shouted Narfi, arm raised.

"To the kitchens!" the other two shouted back.

The adults joined the children as they prepared and ate their favorite foods until they thought they would burst. Loki and Sigyn were amused to see their sons help Jorda clear away and wash the dishes and cooking utensils. They all sat at the table, pleased to have each other's company once again. They soon grew quiet, each lost in his or her own memory of their recent adventures.

Sigyn took Narfi's hands in her own. "Tell us what happened. Did you really go to all the Realms? Even Niflheim and Helheim?" she asked.

"Helheim wasn't so bad," began Narfi. "Hela demanded we promise her our birthdays to get us out, however. Niflheim wasn't much fun."

"Had to ride Yggdrasil's veins back to the room," offered Vali. "Muspellsheim was pretty awful. I had to slay a fire-maned lion to save Jorda. Narfi was brilliant, though. He tricked Surt into sending us all back by offering to stay as hostage while Jorda and I were to go back to retrieve the Warlock's Eye. He made him swear not to leave any part of us behind, and since Narfi and I are identical, he wound up returning with us."

"Jorda befriended a Dwarf in Svartalfaheim and saved us from there. Vali carried me out after I punctured a lung…"

Narfi was stopped by his mother's gasp. "Punctured lung!" Sigyn covered her mouth as if to suppress a scream. Eyes welling, she cupped her youngest son's face. "You were gone but a few hours. We had no idea…" She choked on her own emotions.

Narfi took her hands in his. "It's all right, Mother. We brought all of this on ourselves. You had no way of knowing. But we're here now, and we're fine. I've no ill effects at all. In fact, the memory grows dimmer the more we speak of it. Please don't cry," Narfi tried to reassure his mother.

"My brave, brave sons," she cried. Sigyn took Vali's hand, and continued, "Please swear to me you will not embark on so foolish an adventure again!"

"You know that's not going to happen, woman," interjected Loki. "They are their father's sons. It is in their nature." He stood behind the twins, a hand on their shoulders. "They have learned much from all of this. They know they can face great hardships. They know they have strength and endurance and can work as a team. They know that I will peel their skin from their bones, reattach it, and skin them again if they ever do anything to cause their mother so much anxiety again. Isn't that right, boys?" He smiled down at them.

Jorda leaned into Vali and whispered, "He's kidding, of course?"

Vali hesitated, and then replied, "I'm really not sure." He smiled warily back up at his father.

"You needn't have worried about them." The sudden appearance of Syr in the kitchen doorway startled them all. "I saw that they were in no mortal danger. On the ship, I was the young bride that gave you the date that led you to recall the fate of the Titanic. Hela was expecting you. Your birthdays are safe. Like her father, she enjoys a little mischief herself now and again."

The twins and Jorda looked at one another. "Niflheim?"

"The furs and bones. You were clever to think of the roots of Yggdrasil, Jorda. I was prepared to find a way to lead you there had you not thought of it on your own. I was not needed in Jotunheim. Angrboda took good care of you. Those who know your father best have a…" She searched for the words. "A great and lasting affection for him. I was surprised that Fenrir agreed to help you. You should maintain your relationship with him. He still has a good heart."

Loki stared hard at the Norn they knew as Syr. "You created the portal. You put my sons and this innocent girl through all of this misery and pain. I would like to know why?" he demanded.

"Oh, chill out, Loki. I knew of Freya's plans to defeat Asgard, and some of the paths indicated she would, in fact, win. I could not allow this to happen, but I could not change the path myself. I saw in one path that your sons eventually defeated Frey and Freya in battle, but only after the loss of thousands of lives. I prepared the room of doors for them to harden them for battle, should it come to that so the war might end sooner. They needed to trust their own strengths, without their magic. I taught them something of Asgard's history, some of their own history, and how to make the right friends and to depend on one another. I saw new paths opening as they overcame each obstacle in each Realm. I came to Jorda as Galvi, and helped get Narfi to the healers of Vanaheim. And when Freya seduced Narfi…" Another gasp from Sigyn stopped her short, then she continued, "Sorry, my dear, but he is well of age. He is older than Loki was when you and he…"

Sigyn, wide eyed, gave Syr a small, but violent shake of her head.

Syr brought her hand up to her mouth. "Oh, yes, sorry, dear." She smiled a wry smile at Sigyn and then Loki. "Where was I? Oh, yes. When she took Narfi and sent the others on without him, I knew she had made a fatal mistake.

She wanted to hurt Loki, but she underestimated his intelligence. As soon as Vali and Jorda reentered Asgard, all the paths showed her defeat. I am sorry for the pain your children endured, but as Narfi indicated, the memory fades. Soon, all you will have are the tales of your great strengths and victories to recall. The pain should be as a footnote."

Loki was still displeased. "This all seems like a very roundabout way to stop a war," he said.

"All the truly effective ways to stop war are, dear Loki. Wars are stopped every day. If the methods were obvious, it would blow your mind how many close calls there have been. Relax. It's like one of your own little pranks--all's well that ends well." She actually giggled.

Loki ran a hand over his face but smiled at her. "And you had to use my sons for your little prank?" he asked.

"Of course, my dear. They are Loki's sons!"

The End.